Unconsciously Alive
A Journey into the Unknown

Bhumika Goswami

Ukiyoto Publishing

All global publishing rights are held by

Ukiyoto Publishing

Published in 2024

Content Copyright © **Bhumika Goswami**

ISBN 9789367951118

All rights reserved.
No part of this publication may be reproduced, transmitted, or stored in a retrieval system, in any form by any means, electronic, mechanical, photocopying, recording or otherwise, without the prior permission of the publisher.

The moral rights of the author have been asserted.

This is a work of fiction. Names, characters, businesses, places, events, locales, and incidents are either the products of the author's imagination or used in a fictitious manner. Any resemblance to actual persons, living or dead, or actual events is purely coincidental.

This book is sold subject to the condition that it shall not by way of trade or otherwise, be lent, resold, hired out or otherwise circulated, without the publisher's prior consent, in any form of binding or cover other than that in which it is published.

www.ukiyoto.com

*"Every morning, we are born again.
What we do today is what matters most."*

Acknowledgement

I want to express my deepest gratitude to ***You.***

The readers!

To each one of you who believes in the magic of simply *living*. Who understands that life, though exhausting at times, has a way of stirring the soul, guiding you through fleeting moments of thought, wonder, and inspiration.

This is for those who believe in themselves—their individuality, quirks, strengths, and imperfections alike. For those who embrace their unique essence, in both light and shadow.

Here's to ***Acceptance*** —a journey that may not always be easy, but one that is undeniably worth it. Cheers to you, for choosing to live, believe, and simply *be*.

CONTENTS

Chapter 1 - The Cave and the Palace   1

Chapter 2 - The Keeper   13

Chapter 3 - Through the Painting   21

Chapter 4 - The Journey Ahead   31

Chapter 5 - A Symphony of Awakening   41

Chapter 6 - Trials Ahead   47

Chapter 7 - Bonds of Friendship   57

Chapter 8 - Shadows of the Unknown   69

Chapter 9 - Into the Light   77

Chapter 10 - The Chants of Power   87

Chapter 11 - The Gathering Storm   97

Chapter 12 - The Heart of Darkness   107

Chapter 13 - Ancestral Guardians   117

Chapter 14 - The Final Confrontation   127

Chapter 15 - The Dawn of New Beginnings   139

Epilogue   149

A New Beginning   149

About the Author   *156*

Chapter 1
The Cave and the Palace

"How is this even possible?" Ananya whispered, her voice trembling as she glanced down at the heavy armor clinging awkwardly to her frame. The steel gloves felt foreign against her fingers, clumsy and heavy. She fumbled with them, frustration bubbling beneath the surface, and tucked her wild, blackish curls behind her ears—a nervous habit she couldn't quite shake.

"I just remember Mom telling me to go to bed" She tried to recall "She was... yes, she was telling me to shut my laptop down and sleep, I guess I did that... I have just closed my eyes and now I'm in this dark, freaking cave? In armor? What the hell!"

"It's a dream. It's a dream." She started mumbling.

She tried to blink many times in hope of waking up in her room. But Nothing changed. She got anxious.

Ananya's sharp eyes darted around the cave, quickly assessing her surroundings. Despite the fear gnawing at her chest, her fierce spirit refused to let panic take control. She was the kind of person who always found a way—strong, stubborn, and kind, but only when kindness was deserved.

The dim light shimmered off the wet, stone walls, casting jagged shadows. Water dripped in slow, steady beats, each droplet a subtle reminder of their surreal situation. The heavy, humid scent of damp earth filled the air, thick like the smell of the ground after a monsoon storm.

As she tried to walk after gaining consciousness, she saw two shadows. She stumbled.

Careful! She heard two more persons.

Two strangers stood beside her, both looking just as lost. They exchanged uncertain glances, each trying to mask their fear—though it lingered, evident in the slight twitch of their eyes and fidgeting hands.

"So..." Ananya began awkwardly, rubbing the back of her armored glove on her thigh. She hated silences. They made her feel like everything might fall apart if she didn't say something—anything. "I'm Ananya. And you guys are?"

The taller of the two gave a small, tired smile. His blue eyes, soft and observant, seemed oddly calm given the situation. There was a tranquility to him, a quiet acceptance that things were beyond his control. His fair skin glowed faintly in the dim light, and his sandy brown hair fell messily over his forehead. Andrew was a steady presence—someone you wanted around in a crisis, not because he knew the answers, but because he wouldn't let panic cloud his actions.

"I'm Andrew," he said with a slight shrug, rubbing the back of his neck. "Hey..." His voice was low and measured, like someone used to waiting for the right moment to speak.

The other boy shifted his weight nervously. He was smaller, compact, with soft brown eyes that sparkled with both curiosity and unease. His dark hair stuck up in wild tufts, as if he'd been running his hands through it repeatedly. Asim's presence carried a certain boyish charm—sweet, goofy, and genuine to the core. He seems kind, the kind of person who could make you laugh even when things looked bleak. But right now, his nervous energy was palpable.

"Asim," he muttered, scratching his arm. "Uh... sorry. This is weird, right? I mean, I remember falling asleep at my place, and now—well—here we are." His words tumbled out awkwardly, like he was thinking aloud more than speaking to them. "Do you guys feel that? Like... we're not supposed to be here, but at the same time, it kinda feels... right?" He gave a lopsided grin, his attempt at humor thin, but endearing.

Ananya gave a half-smile in response. "Yeah, Asim, it's weird. But I guess we'll figure it out." The fierceness in her voice hinted at her determination to do just that—figure it out, no matter what.

Andrew leaned back slightly, taking in the other two. "Okay," he said in his calm, steady voice, "whatever this is, it looks like we're in it together."

Ananya, fierce and ready to fight whatever came their way; Andrew, calm and grounded, someone to lean on when things got tough; and Asim, goofy and lighthearted, a reminder that even in the darkest places, there was room for laughter.

The silence stretched again, but this time, it wasn't uncomfortable. It was the quiet kind of understanding that comes when people know they'll have to rely on each other, whether they want to or not.

Ananya nodded grimly. "Yeah, same here. But sitting around isn't going to help. It's stuffy in here, and I can't breathe in this armor. Let's find a way out."

Ananya took a deep breath, her hand drifting instinctively to the hilt of a sword strapped to her side. "Okay," she said. "Let's find out what's going on."

The three exchanged brief, uncertain glances but gave each other quick nods. Without speaking, they set off down the only visible path, a narrow corridor that twisted deeper into the shadows of the cave. Their footsteps echoed against the damp walls, the sloshing sound of water dripping amplifying the unease creeping through their minds. Each step forward was a mixture of excitement and fear, like standing at the edge of a cliff—not knowing whether they'd fly or fall if they jumped.

As they walked, the weight of their situation pressed down on them. Their breaths were shallow, hearts racing—not entirely from fear, but from the strange thrill of not knowing what lay ahead. Ananya clenched and unclenched her fists inside her gauntlets, her pulse drumming in her ears. She could feel her armor shifting with each step, still awkward on her body, but it made her feel... powerful. The same power, however, came with a gnawing discomfort: Why was she here? And what was waiting for them at the end of the path?

Andrew walked silently, stealing quick glances at the others as if trying to gauge how they were holding up. His calm demeanor wasn't effortless; it was a choice—an anchor to keep them from being swept away by the chaos of their thoughts. He had been through some strange things in life, but this was on another level entirely. Still, a flicker of excitement stirred inside him. For some reason, it felt like the beginning of an adventure.

Asim was trying to make light of it, but his jokes came out flat. He fidgeted constantly, running his hands through his messy hair or tapping his fingers on his thighs. His nervous energy made it hard for him to stay still, but beneath it all, there was a strange sense of exhilaration—like a kid sneaking into a forbidden playground. Sure, it was terrifying, but it was also... cool.

After several tense minutes of trudging through darkness, a flicker of light ahead caught their attention. It was faint at first, just a distant shimmer, but it made all their hearts race.

"There! Look!" Andrew's voice rang out, more energetic than it had been since they started. The thrill of finding something—anything—felt like a lifeline in the darkness.

They bolted toward the light, adrenaline pumping through their veins. The cave walls blurred as they ran, the cold air biting at their skin. It was exhilarating—like sprinting through the final stretch of a race, fueled by a mixture of hope, fear, and uncertainty.

When they burst through the opening, the sudden flood of brightness blinded them. They stumbled to a halt, shielding their eyes from the dazzling light. But as their vision adjusted, the sight before them took their breath away.

A magnificent palace loomed in the distance, its golden spires gleaming under a brilliant sky, as if they had stepped into a dream. Vast green fields stretched out in all directions, alive with the songs of unseen birds. A soft breeze carried the fragrance of blooming flowers, making the moment feel surreal.

"It's... magnificent," Ananya whispered, her shock slowly giving way to wonder. Her heart swelled with awe—she had never seen anything like this. It was beautiful, magical, and impossibly strange, all at once.

Asim let out a startled laugh, the sound like a sudden burst of joy breaking the tension. "This looks straight out of a fairy tale. Like... Hogwarts!"

Andrew chuckled, shaking his head. "Yeah, this is unreal." For a moment, their worries seemed to melt away, replaced by the simple thrill of discovery.

They ventured across the field, following a narrow path that led toward the palace gates. Ananya, however, couldn't quite shake the knot of unease coiled in her stomach. As she walked, she kept glancing over her shoulder, her brows knitting together.

"You okay?" Andrew asked, noticing her hesitation.

"I just... felt something," she admitted, scanning the bushes behind them. Her pulse quickened, her instincts prickling with warning. "It's like... someone's watching us."

"What, you think someone's following us?" Asim teased, though there was a nervous edge to his voice.

"Maybe..." Ananya muttered. "Probably just my imagination, though. This has to be a dream, right?"

Andrew gave her a skeptical look. "If it's a dream, how come we're all having the same one? None of us know each other."

Asim grinned nervously. "Good point. But maybe if we just play along, we'll wake up, and all of this will go away." He laughed again, trying to push away the unease curling at the back of his mind.

They reached the towering gates, which swung open with an eerie groan as they stepped inside. The palace was even more breathtaking up close. The walls were adorned with sculptures that seemed to come alive in the flickering light, and chandeliers sparkled like constellations suspended from the ceiling. Intricate patterns wove across the marble floors, making it feel like they had entered a place from another world.

"Whoa... this place is incredible!" Asim exclaimed, his voice echoing through the vast hallways. They laughed, excitement bubbling over like children exploring a magical wonderland for the first time. For a brief, blissful moment, the fear that had shadowed them vanished, replaced by childlike joy.

They ran through the halls, racing and exploring, their laughter bouncing off the walls. Ananya's heart felt lighter than it had in ages. The thrill of adventure, the beauty around them—it was intoxicating, making them forget, just for a moment, that they didn't belong here.

But then... the laughter stopped.

Ananya slowed to a halt, a chill running down her spine. The air had shifted—gone was the warmth, replaced by a creeping stillness. The joy she had felt just moments ago evaporated, leaving behind a gnawing sense of dread.

She spun around, her pulse spiking. "Andrew? Asim?" she called out, her voice bouncing down the empty corridor.

No answer.

"Come on, guys! This isn't funny!" Her voice cracked, panic beginning to creep in.

She sprinted through the hallways, her heart pounding harder with every step. There was no sign of them—no voices, no footsteps, nothing. It was as if the palace had swallowed them whole.

"Where the hell are you guys?" Ananya whispered, her voice trembling.

Then she heard it—a faint whisper, drifting through the shadows like a breeze that didn't belong.

"Asim? Andrew?" she called again, her voice faltering.

She rounded a corner—and froze. Andrew lay unconscious on the cold marble floor, his chest rising and falling shallowly.

"Andrew!" she cried, rushing to his side. She shook him frantically, her hands trembling, but he didn't stir.

And Asim... was still missing.

"Hello, Ananya..." a voice rasped, low and sinister, slicing through the silence like a knife.

Ananya whipped around, her heart hammering in her chest, but there was no one there.

"Who's there?" she demanded, her voice sharp with fear. "Show yourself!"

The voice chuckled, a dark, smoky sound that seemed to curl around her like a vine. "Temper, temper, child. I'd keep that anger in check if I were you... unless you want to die. Not just in dreams... but in reality."

Ananya's blood ran cold.

"Reality?" she whispered, the word tasting bitter on her tongue.

Could it be true? Was this strange, surreal place more than just a dream?

And most terrifying of all—were they going to die here?

Chapter 2
The Keeper

Ananya felt a burning heat surge through her body, her pulse racing like a bullet train. Her chest tightened, and her palms grew clammy with sweat. One companion was missing, and the other—Andrew—lay cold and pale, lifeless on the marble floor.

Terror gripped her heart, its weight unbearable.

"WHO ARE YOU?" she screamed, her voice cracking under the pressure. Tears welled in her eyes, spilling freely as anxiety clawed at her soul.

"I am the one you'll need to survive this, my dear girl," the voice answered softly.

A chill breeze drifted from the direction of the voice, brushing against Ananya's skin. She sensed movement—someone was coming closer. Her heart pounded in her ears as a shadow began to take shape at the far end of the gallery. Slowly, the shadow transformed into the figure of a woman.

The woman was small, barely five feet tall, with deep wrinkles etched across her face. Yet there was a strange sparkle in her eyes—sharp and knowing. She wore a flowing white kimono trimmed with gold, her presence serene but unsettling. Despite her elderly appearance, her voice carried a youthful resonance.

"Why—why am I here? And who... who are you?" Ananya stammered, her voice trembling as confusion and fear threatened to overwhelm her. She desperately needed answers.

The woman gave a cryptic smile.

"Is this a dream... or reality?" Ananya asked, her words tumbling out in panic. "We're not going to die here, right?"

"My name is Daikichi," the woman replied. "I am the keeper of this place. You are here because you, Andrew, and Asim... are the Oracle's Heirs."

"The Oracle's Heirs?" Ananya repeated, frowning. "What does that even mean?"

"I'll explain everything, but not here," Daikichi said, her expression turning serious. "We don't have much time. **He** is coming for you." She glanced down at Andrew's unconscious form. "He can sense you now."

"How do I know you're not the one behind all this?" Ananya demanded, stepping protectively in front of Andrew. "What if this is a trap? And where is Asim?"

Daikichi took a step closer, her eyes meeting Ananya's with an unnerving calm. "Trust me—just this once," she whispered.

Ananya's instincts screamed at her to run, to fight, to do anything but trust this strange woman. But deep down, she knew she had no other choice. With a reluctant nod, she stepped aside and allowed Daikichi to kneel beside Andrew.

Daikichi knelt by Andrew with an air of quiet authority, her hands moving with practiced precision. There was no hesitation, no malice in her movements. Instead, there was a strange sense of familiarity, as if she had done this many times before. Something about her didn't add up—and yet, beneath all the fear and suspicion, a flicker of calm began to take root in Ananya's mind.

Daikichi took Andrew's cold hand in hers and began chanting in a strange, lilting rhythm.

"Elboraaa misforariii laturrmonaa..."

"Elboraaa misforariii laturrmonaa..."

"Elboraaa misforariii laturrmonaa..."

Andrew's body jerked violently, his limbs trembling as if struck by a powerful current. He let out a bloodcurdling scream that echoed through the palace halls.

"Aaaaaaahhhh!" Andrew shrieked, his eyes snapping open.

He bolted upright, gasping for breath as if he had been drowning moments earlier.

"Andrew! You're awake!" Ananya cried, rushing to him and wrapping her arms around him in relief. "Thank God you're okay!"

Andrew's body shook uncontrollably, his breaths ragged and shallow. "Ananya, we... we need to go!" he stammered, clutching her arm.

"It's okay," Ananya whispered, trying to calm him. "You're fine now."

Ananya's pulse thundered in her ears as fear clawed at her chest, every instinct screaming that this strange, small woman might be a threat. She felt trapped between her confusion and the grim reality before her—Andrew had been cold, lifeless, yet now his eyes were wide with frantic life.

"No, you don't understand!" Andrew gasped, his voice urgent and panicked. "He's coming! I can feel him! We have to trust her—there's no other way!"

"Who's coming?" Ananya asked, her heart pounding harder than ever.

Daikichi stood, her expression grim. "We must leave now. I'll answer your questions later, but Andrew needs rest—and Asim is already waiting in the safe zone."

"Asim's safe?" Ananya asked, her voice tinged with hope.

Daikichi gave a curt nod. "Yes. He's with me."

"But how—"

"No time for explanations here," Daikichi interrupted. "Follow me. If you want to survive, we need to move quickly."

It felt reckless, dangerous even, but the alternative was worse. Running blind through the halls of this nightmare, with no sense of direction or hope, could mean certain death.

Daikichi's steady, unwavering gaze met Ananya's, and for a moment, the chaos inside her stilled. There was something about the woman's eyes—aged but sharp, as if they saw past the moment, past the fear, to something that only she knew. Trustworthy wasn't the right word, but it was close. It was as if Daikichi carried an unshakable truth with her, and though Ananya didn't understand it, she knew she had no other choice but to follow.

Her hand gripped Andrew's tighter. His skin was cold and trembling, but the faint squeeze of his fingers told her he was awake—alive.

With a reluctant exhale, Ananya gave Daikichi a small nod. "We'll follow you," she whispered, though her heart still hammered against her ribs.

Daikichi gave no sign of satisfaction or relief, only a curt nod. "Good. There's no more time to hesitate."

As they moved through the dim corridor, the air thick with shadows and unanswered questions, Ananya felt a strange shift inside herself. She wasn't sure if it was hope or dread—only that with every step they took behind Daikichi, the nagging certainty grew: whatever lay ahead, this woman was the only chance they had to survive.

And somewhere in the silent darkness behind them, the unseen presence continued to stir—watching, waiting.

Ananya helped Andrew to his feet, his legs wobbling beneath him. Together, they followed the mysterious woman down the dim corridor, leaving the eerie silence of the palace behind.

And somewhere in the shadows, **something**—or **someone**—watched. Waiting.

Chapter 3
Through the Painting

Ananya and Andrew followed Daikichi without a word, their steps light yet filled with uncertainty. The silence around them was so profound that every small sound—their breaths, the soft rustle of clothing, and even the faint squeak of Andrew's boots—seemed magnified, as if the palace walls were holding their secrets close and listening intently.

Despite the unsettling quiet, a strange sense of peace hung in the air, as though the place wanted them to relax—wanted them to forget how strange everything was. The tranquility was almost hypnotic, soothing, yet unnerving, like the calm before a storm.

They walked through gallery after gallery, each one more extravagant than the last. The architecture was a marvel, with towering arches carved from ivory-white stone and pillars engraved with ancient symbols. Sunlight streamed through the high stained-glass windows, casting a kaleidoscope of colors that shimmered like a dream across the polished marble floors.

The walls were adorned with paintings of kings, queens, and mythical creatures, their gazes hauntingly lifelike, as though they could step out of the frames at any moment. Gold-framed mirrors, massive chandeliers dripping with crystals, and strange relics—daggers, scrolls, and masks—were scattered throughout the galleries, each hinting at a forgotten history.

Andrew leaned closer to Ananya as they walked. "She's pretty fast for someone her age, don't you think?" he whispered, his voice tinged with disbelief.

Ananya shot him a sharp look. "Focus. We don't know what we're dealing with."

Daikichi led them deeper into the palace, her movements purposeful and quick. Suddenly, she came to a halt in front of a massive painting—a serene, idyllic scene of a mother and her children feeding a flock of white sheep. The brushstrokes were so soft and precise that the figures looked as though they might blink or smile at any moment.

Without a word, Daikichi lifted her hands and began to chant under her breath, her fingers tracing intricate, invisible patterns over the painting's surface. Her whispers flowed like a delicate song carried by the wind, the words impossible to grasp, slipping away just as Ananya and Andrew thought they might understand.

Andrew squinted, his brows furrowed. "What's she saying? Can you hear it?"

"No. But it feels... ancient," Ananya whispered, an involuntary shiver running down her spine.

Just as suddenly as she had started, Daikichi stopped and turned toward them, her expression unreadable. "Follow me."

Andrew raised an eyebrow. "Follow you? Into a painting?"

Without waiting for a reply, Daikichi stepped forward—and melted into the canvas, her form vanishing into the serene landscape like a ripple on water.

Andrew's eyes widened in disbelief. "Did you just see that?"

Ananya rolled her eyes, the surreal nature of the situation no longer surprising her. "Yeah. You missed a lot while you were passed out."

Andrew threw his hands up in frustration. "I'm not going in there! This feels like... some kind of weird magic!"

"Seriously?" Ananya crossed her arms and glared at him. "You'd rather stay here and faint again? Asim might be waiting on the other side. And besides, we need answers."

Andrew groaned, running a hand through his hair. "Fine. But this is officially the weirdest day of my life."

"Welcome to the club," Ananya muttered, grabbing his arm.

Together, they stepped forward—and the painting swallowed them whole.

On the other side, the air was cooler, damp with the scent of earth and stone. They stood in a narrow tunnel, dimly lit by the soft glow of a green lantern in Daikichi's hand. Shadows danced across the walls, giving the impression that the stones themselves were breathing.

"Keep close," Daikichi instructed, her voice crisp. "We can't afford to waste time."

The ground beneath their feet was uneven, a mixture of wet rock and ancient stone steps, slick with moisture. Ananya and Andrew followed in silence, their shoes splashing in shallow puddles.

Andrew grumbled under his breath, struggling to keep up with Daikichi's brisk pace. "How is she moving so fast? And where did she even get that lantern?"

"Do I look like I know?" Ananya hissed back, annoyed but just as curious.

As they trudged through the winding tunnel, the rough terrain gradually smoothed out, the rocky path giving way to wooden planks and scattered crates. The walls were lined with old barrels, trunks, and broken tools—remnants of a long-abandoned storeroom.

"This is the safest route," Daikichi said without looking back. "Remember it well. If anything goes wrong, this path will lead you back to safety."

"How much farther?" Ananya asked, her heart racing with a mix of exhaustion and anticipation.

"We're almost there," Daikichi replied calmly. "Just a few more steps."

They pressed forward, the darkness thinning ahead of them. A soft, golden light beckoned them from the tunnel's end, and soon they stepped out into a world that seemed too perfect to be real.

The sight that greeted them was breathtaking.

A sprawling meadow stretched out before them, alive with vibrant colors—wildflowers in every shade imaginable, their petals swaying gently in the breeze. A crystal-clear stream meandered through the fields, its water sparkling like a thousand tiny diamonds under the sun.

Children laughed and played in the distance, their voices mingling with the soft murmur of the wind. Adults gathered under the shade of massive trees, sharing stories and bread, their faces lit with joy. Animals grazed peacefully—sheep, cows, and horses dotted the landscape, moving lazily across the meadows.

Andrew blinked, stunned by the scene. "This... this is incredible. Definitely not witchcraft."

Ananya smiled, her heart lifting as she took in the beauty around her. For the first time since their strange journey began, she felt a flicker of hope. "It's... beautiful," she whispered.

Then, remembering why they had followed Daikichi, she turned to her. "Where's Asim? You said he's here."

Daikichi gave a knowing smile. "He is. Right where he should be."

Before Ananya could ask what that meant, a familiar voice rang out across the meadow.

"ANANYA! ANDREW! Over here!"

Their heads snapped toward the sound—and just in time to see Asim sprinting toward them, his face lit with joy.

"Asim!" Ananya cried, her voice breaking with relief.

Before they could react, Asim tackled Andrew in a playful hug, laughing as he clung to him. "I thought I'd never see you guys again!"

Andrew stumbled back, but a wide grin spread across his face. "You and me both, man."

Ananya joined the embrace, tears of relief stinging her eyes. For the first time since their terrifying ordeal began, the weight on her heart lifted. They were together again.

And whatever lay ahead, they would face it as a team— no matter how strange or dangerous this world might be.

From the shadows at the far edge of the meadow, Daikichi watched them silently, a faint smile playing on her lips. They were safe... for now. But the journey was far from over.

Something unseen still lurked in the distance— watching, waiting, preparing.

Chapter 4
The Journey Ahead

Sometimes, life can feel overwhelmingly difficult. It may seem like everything is shattering around you, pieces scattering in all directions. But little do we know—it is nature's law to break us, only to reshape us into something more beautiful, a design we cannot yet understand.

As Ananya, Asim, and Andrew stood before Daikichi, their hearts thudding with the fear of the unknown. The weight of their mission pressed heavily on their minds, making it impossible to relax despite the exhaustion in their bones. And just when they thought they could ask the questions spinning in their heads, a figure emerged from the shadows.

"Meet Adam," Daikichi announced, her soft voice cutting through the silence. "Our finest soldier. He will guide you on the journey that lies ahead. Rest tonight—at first light, you must move."

Adam nodded, his sharp gray eyes assessing the trio in one swift glance. His towering frame and the scar across his cheek suggested a life spent on battlefields. His presence was both reassuring and unsettling—like a storm waiting for the right moment to strike.

The three exchanged anxious glances. Fear twisted in their chests, not just of the dangers ahead, but of the ticking clock counting down their borrowed time in this strange world.

"How are we supposed to sleep?" Asim muttered. "You said the sunlight could kill us. What if we don't wake up?"

Daikichi smiled gently, her eyes filled with both wisdom and sadness. "Fear not, child. This realm is different from yours. Here, time flows like a river through a dream. Every thirty minutes in your world equals a full day here. So, for every twenty-four hours that pass for you, forty-eight days pass in this land."

Andrew's brow furrowed. "That sounds… confusing. But wait, how does that help us?"

Daikichi's smile deepened, as though she was about to reveal the piece of a puzzle they hadn't even known existed. "Your presence here is no accident. You were chosen—not by chance, but by design." She stepped closer, her gaze fixed on each of them in turn.

"In every century, the universe selects three souls, scattered across different realms, bound by time yet connected by destiny. You three—Ananya, Asim, and Andrew—were born under stars that aligned in perfect coordinates across your respective time zones, forming a triangle of immense cosmic power."

The trio exchanged baffled looks. Ananya leaned forward, intrigued but skeptical. "What do you mean… a triangle?"

Daikichi's voice softened, carrying the weight of prophecy. "Three individuals—each from a different corner of the world, from exact geographic locations, connected by time zones that overlap perfectly. When these three souls come together, they create a triangle capable of channeling energy beyond human comprehension. It is said that such a triangle can alter fate, reshape reality, and awaken ancient forces lying dormant."

She gestured toward them as if revealing a great secret. "You are that triangle."

For a moment, no one spoke. The fire crackled softly, sending embers spiraling into the night. The gravity of Daikichi's words settled over the group like a heavy cloak.

"So... we're some kind of cosmic superheroes?" Andrew asked with a weak grin, trying to break the tension.

Daikichi chuckled softly. "Not quite. Your power does not lie in muscle or magic—it lies in harmony. Only by uniting your minds, hearts, and spirits will the triangle's true power awaken."

Ananya crossed her arms, her mind racing. "If we're so powerful, why do we only have twelve days to complete this mission?"

"The triangle's power is fragile," Daikichi explained. "It strengthens over time but can be easily broken if doubt, fear, or discord enter your hearts. And the window of time you have—those twelve days—is the only moment the universe allows for this convergence. If you fail to complete your task within that time, the triangle will dissolve, and the world you stand in will be lost forever."

Asim exhaled, rubbing the back of his neck. "No pressure then. Just save the world before the clock runs out."

"It's more than that," Daikichi added gravely. "If the three of you are not perfectly aligned—if even one of you falters—the triangle's energy will collapse. And so will your fates."

The trio exchanged uncertain glances. The task ahead of them had seemed daunting before, but now it felt monumental.

Asim glanced at the sky, anxiety creeping in. "Wait... You said Ananya's time zone is first, right? That means her sun rises before ours, she has six hours less." He paused, doing the math aloud. "That gives us only twelve days—twelve days to save the world and ourselves."

"And if we fail?" Ananya asked, her voice low.

"If you fail," Daikichi whispered, her eyes darkening, "you will return to your world... just in time to watch it crumble."

The fire crackled again, filling the heavy silence. Andrew rubbed his temples, feeling the weight of the prophecy settle on his shoulders. "So... no pressure at all," he muttered, half-joking but fully aware of the looming danger.

Ananya shook her head, a determined glint in her eye. "We can't afford to fail. We need a plan—and we need rest. If we're going to save this world, we'll have to do it together."

Adam, who had been listening silently, stepped forward. "Sleep now," he said gruffly. "You'll need all your strength. The journey ahead won't just test your skills—it will test your bond."

Adam led them to a small clearing where a tent stood waiting, and the warm glow of a fire flickered in the darkness. The group huddled around the flames, their fatigue giving way to the warmth of shared stories.

Ananya spoke of her family and the love she carried with her, even in this strange world. Asim shared tales of his childhood in the bustling streets of his hometown, while Andrew, always the jokester, told them about his misadventures at boarding school.

Their laughter filled the night, chasing away the shadows of fear.

Adam leaned in closer, his expression turning serious. "Have you ever heard the legend of the Greater Power of Three?" he asked quietly.

The trio shook their heads, curious.

"It's an ancient tale," Adam explained. "When three souls from different realms unite, they form a bond stronger than any force in the universe. Together, they can wield a power capable of bending time, rewriting fate, and facing even the darkest of forces."

The three people exchanged glances. For the first time, hope flickered within them. Maybe—just maybe—they were destined for this.

The night passed quietly, and one by one, they drifted into sleep. Their dreams were strange—filled with swirling colors, mysterious symbols, and whispers they could not quite understand.

Morning arrived with the first golden light filtering through the trees. Birds sang in the distance, and a soft breeze stirred the leaves. Adam was already awake, packing supplies with swift, practiced hands.

"Time to move," he announced. "We have a long road ahead."

They set off through the forest, following narrow trails winding through vibrant green fields. The air was crisp, and for a moment, the beauty of the landscape made them forget the danger they were in.

But as they ventured deeper into the woods, a chill crept down Ananya's spine. She glanced over her shoulder, her heart racing.

"Do you feel that?" she whispered to Asim, walking beside her.

He frowned. "Feel what?"

"Like we're being watched," she murmured, her voice barely audible.

Andrew nodded in agreement. "I've been feeling it too... like something's following us."

Adam's eyes darkened. "Stay close," he warned, his hand resting on the hilt of his dagger. "And keep your senses sharp. We're not alone."

The path grew darker, the air thick with tension. Shadows flickered at the edge of their vision, and a low growl echoed from the depths of the forest.

The journey had truly begun—and the triangle of fate was about to be tested in ways they could never imagine.

Chapter 5
A Symphony of Awakening

As the first light of dawn painted the forest in gold, Ananya, Asim, and Andrew followed Adam through a winding path that seemed to dance with life. The chill of the night was replaced by the warmth of the rising sun, and the landscape unfurled before them—a vibrant tapestry of meadows, streams, and trees that shimmered as if kissed by magic.

The trail carried them along the edge of a cliff, where a magnificent waterfall cascaded down into a crystalline pool. The sound of rushing water echoed like a soothing lullaby, and droplets sparkled mid-air, reflecting the sunlight in iridescent rainbows.

Ananya paused at the edge, captivated by the scene. "It's like the world's been wrapped in poetry," she whispered, her voice filled with wonder.

The group made their way down to the base of the waterfall, where they found a hidden alcove behind the curtain of water—a sanctuary untouched by time. They dipped their hands into the cool stream, feeling the weight of their mission momentarily lift with each ripple. For a brief moment, the danger felt distant, as if the land itself was inviting them to savor these small, perfect moments.

As they pressed onward, the forest opened into a meadow where flowers swayed like dancers in the breeze, their petals in hues of lavender, amber, and sapphire. Birds with brilliant plumage—blues, reds, and greens—flitted between branches, their songs blending into a harmonious melody.

A particularly curious bird, with shimmering golden feathers, landed on Andrew's shoulder, tilting its head in greeting. Andrew grinned and whispered, "I think this one likes me."

Asim chuckled. "Finally, someone who finds your jokes tolerable."

The bird chirped in response, and they laughed, their spirits lightening with every step.

The group journeyed deeper into the wilderness, encountering animals both familiar and fantastical. A pair of elegant deer, their antlers glowing faintly with an otherworldly light, watched them from the underbrush. At a stream, a family of otters splashed playfully, as if oblivious to the weight of fate carried by the travelers.

But the most enchanting encounter came when they reached a glade filled with glowing butterflies. Their wings shimmered in the twilight, casting soft glimmers of light as they drifted lazily through the air. Ananya stretched out her hand, and a delicate butterfly landed on her palm, its wings pulsing gently as if breathing with her.

"They're like tiny dreams floating through the air," she whispered.

That evening, as the sun dipped low on the horizon, they camped by a tranquil lake surrounded by towering trees. The sky above them became a canvas splattered with stars, each one reflecting on the still surface of the water.

Adam built a small fire, and they gathered around it, the warmth seeping into their tired limbs. The crackling flames seemed to sync with the rhythm of their hearts—three beats, perfectly in harmony.

Asim pulled out a small notebook, drawing rough sketches of the animals they had met that day. "I think this is my favorite part of the journey so far," he said, holding up a quick sketch of the glowing butterflies.

"Mine too," Ananya agreed softly. "It's strange... everything we've seen, it feels like a gift. Like the world is telling us to enjoy this beauty before the real challenge begins. Or before we wakes up."

Andrew leaned back on his elbows, gazing up at the stars. "Or maybe it's a reminder," he mused. "That even when things get tough, there's always something beautiful waiting, just around the corner."

Adam, who had been silent most of the day, finally spoke. "The land rewards those who tread it with purpose," he said quietly. "It gives you beauty, to remind you what you're fighting for."

The words lingered in the night air, heavy with truth. They knew their journey would not remain this peaceful, but in that moment, they allowed themselves to rest. To breathe. To hope.

"The journey ahead will be hard," she whispered to herself.

And with that thought warming her heart, the group continued forward—through sunlit fields and enchanted woods, with waterfalls whispering stories of old and glowing creatures lighting their path.

Chapter 6
Trials Ahead

Confusion and fear clung to Ananya like a shroud as she stirred from a restless slumber. Beads of cold sweat dotted her brow, and her heart thudded dully in her chest as fragmented dreams dissolved into the misty morning. Pushing aside the fabric of the tent, she stepped into the open.

For a brief moment, the breathtaking panorama of the strange land washed away the lingering unease. The sky was painted in hues of lavender, rose, and gold, as if nature herself had crafted a masterpiece for this dawn. Dew-kissed blades of grass shimmered in the soft light, tiny diamonds that sparkled underfoot.

The air was crisp, carrying with it the scent of pine and fresh earth, and the songs of unseen birds created a melodic chorus that floated through the stillness.

For an instant, she forgot the surreal world she had been thrust into, her fear dissolving into the beauty of the morning.

Then, like a clap of thunder cracking through a serene sky, a voice shattered the peace—

"Down Down!"

Ananya's heart seized. Instinct kicked in before reason, and she dropped to her knees just as an arrow hissed past, grazing her ear. It embedded itself into the ground with a dull thud.

"What the—?" she gasped, her breath catching as her wide eyes traced the arrow's path.

"Get down!" Adam's voice sliced through the air, sharp and urgent.

More arrows followed—sharp, whistling threats that cut through the morning silence. The atmosphere shifted in an instant from tranquility to chaos, thick with danger.

Ananya's pulse hammered in her ears as she rolled behind the tent, barely escaping another arrow that sliced through the fabric. She spotted Andrew, who was already crouching behind the tent pole, his expression just as bewildered as hers.

"What in the world is happening?!" she exclaimed, her voice shaking with fear and confusion.

Before she could get a response, Adam darted toward them, a blur of motion as arrows rained down from all sides. His hand was steady and sure as he shoved weapons into their arms—a spear for Ananya, a sword for Andrew, and a quiver of arrows for Asim, who had just scrambled into position beside them.

"Choose!" Adam ordered, his voice unwavering and fierce, his eyes scanning the treetops for the unseen archers.

The trio hesitated, uncertainty flickering in their eyes.

"Why did you choose these weapons for us?" Ananya asked, her voice tinged with confusion.

Adam's eyes sparkled with a hint of mystery. "These weapons did not simply choose me; they resonate with each of you on a deeper level. They were waiting for their true wielders, and your arrival has awakened them."

Ananya's fingers brushed the shaft of the spear, and she felt a warm pulse beneath her touch, as if the weapon itself was alive. A surge of energy coursed through her, filling her with an instinctive sense of purpose.

Asim, grasping the bow, felt a connection that was almost electric. "It's like it's speaking to me," he murmured, a look of wonder crossing his face. "I can sense its power."

Andrew held the sword firmly, its blade gleaming under the morning light. He felt a rush of confidence, a primal instinct awakening within him. "This feels... right," he said, his voice steadying.

"Good," Adam affirmed, a hint of a smile playing on his lips. "Each weapon channels your inner strength, revealing your potential as you learn to wield them. They resonate with your very essence."

The tension thickened as twenty men emerged from the forest, faces concealed beneath dark hoods. They surrounded the group, bows drawn, their footsteps soundless on the grass.

"Why are they attacking us?!" Ananya cried, panic rising like bile in her throat.

"Trust me!" Adam barked, his gaze never wavering from the advancing attackers.

The cold wood of the spear grounded Ananya, and she clutched it with trembling hands. Fear threatened to paralyze her, but a spark of determination flickered deep within. She planted her feet, gripping the spear tightly until her knuckles whitened.

Andrew, with a wild gleam in his eye, adjusted his grip on the sword. "Well," he muttered, "if we're going down, I'm going down swinging." He brandished the weapon awkwardly but with surprising resolve.

Asim nocked an arrow and squinted down its shaft, struggling to calm his breath as his fingers trembled against the bowstring.

"Believe in your weapons," Adam said firmly. "They aren't just tools—they chose you. You are capable of far more than you think."

With that, Adam became a blur of deadly precision, tearing arrows from the air with his bare hands, snapping them like twigs. His movements were fluid and calculated, an effortless dance between attack and defense that left the others speechless.

The attackers surged forward, bows discarded as they drew daggers and swords.

Ananya's focus narrowed. Time seemed to slow as her senses sharpened—every heartbeat, every footstep, every rustle of leaves registered with crystal clarity. Then she saw it: an arrow hurtling toward Asim, who was too preoccupied to notice.

"No!" she screamed, adrenaline surging through her veins. Without thinking, she sprang forward, the spear a natural extension of her body. In one swift, fluid motion, she sliced through the arrow mid-flight, the wood splintering into harmless pieces.

"What?! Did I just... do that?" she gasped, staring at the broken arrow in disbelief.

Adam grinned. "Yes. And you'll do much more."

Andrew, emboldened by Ananya's sudden prowess, swung his sword with newfound confidence. The weapon felt natural in his grip, as if it had been waiting for him all along. He blocked an attacker's blow and countered with a swift slash, his movements strangely precise for someone who had never wielded a sword before.

Meanwhile, Asim released arrow after arrow with growing accuracy. His shots found their mark effortlessly—each arrow embedding itself into an enemy's armor, forcing them to retreat.

The trio fought as one, their strengths aligning as if they had trained together for years. Ananya's spear danced through the air with graceful precision, blocking attacks and striking down enemies. Andrew swung his sword in arcs of silver, each blow landing with calculated force. Asim, from the shadows, loosed arrows that flew with pinpoint accuracy, felling attackers before they even reached the camp.

The tide of the battle shifted. The attackers, once confident, began to falter under the trio's coordinated assault. One by one, they fell, their dark forms crumpling to the ground.

The last of the attackers collapsed with a final, pained grunt. Silence descended over the clearing, broken only by the ragged breaths of the three companions. The battlefield was littered with broken arrows, discarded weapons, and fallen enemies.

Ananya leaned on her spear, her chest heaving as she tried to catch her breath. Andrew wiped the sweat from his brow, a grin spreading across his face despite the fatigue.

"We did it..." he whispered in disbelief, exchanging astonished glances with Ananya and Asim.

Adam approached, his expression calm but filled with pride. "Good," he said simply, as if they had passed a test they hadn't even known they were taking.

"That was a test?" Ananya demanded, still catching her breath, her voice tinged with irritation.

Adam gave a small, knowing smile. "A necessary one. The real challenges lie ahead, and you needed to awaken your instincts."

Andrew sheathed his sword with a dramatic sigh. "Well, I hope the next challenge involves fewer arrows and more snacks."

Ananya shot him a withering look. "This isn't a game, Andrew. We need to be ready for anything."

Asim nodded, still holding his bow. "She's right. If that was just a test, I don't want to know what the real fight looks like."

Adam's gaze darkened. "It will be unlike anything you've ever faced." He paused, his voice turning grave. "But remember this: you are here for a reason. Your strength lies not just in your weapons but in each other. Together, you can alter the fate of this world."

The weight of his words settled over them like a heavy mantle. The gravity of their mission became clearer—it wasn't just about survival; it was about fulfilling a destiny they had only begun to comprehend.

The trio stood in silence, their gazes locked on Adam. They had survived their first challenge, but deep down, they knew this was only the beginning. More trials awaited, and the road ahead would demand everything they had—and more.

They exchanged determined glances. Together, they would face whatever lay ahead. Together, they would fight for the fate of this strange, enchanted world.

Chapter 7
Bonds of Friendship

As the days rolled on in this strange land, Ananya, Asim, and Andrew began to realize that their shared experience was forging a bond far deeper than mere companionship.

Each trial they faced, every victory they achieved, and even their moments of despair knit their hearts together in a way they had never anticipated.

During the nights, as they gathered around a small fire outside their tent, the conversations flowed easily, weaving a tapestry of shared experiences that wrapped around them like a warm blanket.

The crackling fire illuminated their faces, casting flickering shadows that danced along the surrounding trees, and the air was rich with the aroma of roasted roots and herbs.

They shared stories of their lives before this adventure, their dreams, and their fears. These moments of vulnerability became the bedrock of their friendship, a safe space where laughter mingled with heartfelt confessions.

One evening, as the stars twinkled above like scattered diamonds, Asim spoke up, his voice soft but filled with sincerity. "You know, before all of this, I was just a regular kid, glued to my video games and too scared to step outside my comfort zone. I never thought I'd be fighting shadows in a different world."

He chuckled softly, shaking his head, his fingers toying nervously with a small twig. "Now I'm just trying to keep my head above water."

"Trust me, we're all out of our comfort zones," Andrew replied with a warm smile, nudging Asim playfully. "But you've handled the challenges like a pro! That arrow you shot the other day? It was amazing!"

Ananya leaned in, her eyes sparkling with mischief. "Yeah, and who knew you could wield a spear like a warrior? Maybe you should consider taking up arms in the real world!" Her laughter bubbled up, brightening the dimming twilight.

Asim's cheeks flushed, both from embarrassment and pride. "Well, maybe I could. But don't forget, you both helped out too. Andrew, that sword technique was something else!" His admiration for his friends swelled, filling him with a sense of belonging he had never felt before.

Andrew shrugged, his modesty shining through like the flickering flames. "I just did what had to be done. But it felt good, didn't it? Like we were meant to be here, fighting together."

Ananya nodded, her heart swelling with appreciation for the two boys beside her. "It did. And I think we're growing stronger as a team with every challenge. I feel like I can rely on you both, no matter what comes next."

As the fire crackled, they exchanged stories about their families, hopes, and the things they missed from home. Ananya talked about her little brother, a mischievous child who used to make her laugh with his silly antics, recounting tales of how he would pull pranks that made their parents exasperated.

Her eyes misted over, revealing a tender vulnerability as she admitted how much she longed to protect him.

Asim shared his passion for drawing, how he always dreamed of becoming an artist. "I used to spend hours sketching fantastical worlds and characters," he confessed, his voice a mix of nostalgia and yearning. "I never imagined I'd be living in one."

Andrew spoke of his childhood in a coastal town, where he spent hours building sandcastles and dreaming of adventures that always felt just out of reach. His gaze drifted into the distance, the waves of memory washing over him as he recounted the salty breeze and the sound of gulls. "I guess I always wanted to be a hero," he mused.

They were all sitting together. Laughing, gazing each other's smile. Sometimes companionship of likeminded but uniquely different people impacts you more than knowing someone for years.

These moments brought them closer, revealing the intricate threads of their lives that had led them to this point. They began to learn each other's strengths and weaknesses, discovering how to support one another during the difficult days. Laughter echoed around the campfire, mingling with the chirping of crickets, creating a symphony of camaraderie.

One night, after a particularly grueling day of challenges, Ananya noticed Andrew sitting alone, staring into the fire with a furrowed brow. She approached him quietly, the warmth of the fire contrasting with the cool night air. "Hey, you okay?"

He looked up, his eyes reflecting the flickering flames, revealing a storm of thoughts beneath the calm exterior. "Just... thinking. I can't help but wonder what happens if we fail. What if we don't defeat the Shadow?"

Ananya sat down beside him, her presence comforting. "We're not going to fail. We have each other, and we've already come so far. Remember what Adam said? We're the Oracle's Heirs for a reason."

Andrew nodded slowly, but doubt still lingered in his eyes. "Yeah, but what if that reason isn't enough?"

"Then we'll make it enough," Ananya said firmly, her voice unwavering. "Together, we're stronger. We've proven that time and again. Besides, we're not just fighting for ourselves; we're fighting for everyone in this kingdom."

Her words seemed to resonate with him, igniting a flicker of hope. "You're right. Thanks, Ananya. I needed to hear that."

As the days passed, the trio found themselves sharing laughter amidst the challenges, forging an unbreakable bond. They learned to strategize together, leaning on one another's strengths to overcome their weaknesses.

When it came time for training, they practiced together, pushing each other to improve. Ananya discovered she had a natural gift for strategy, able to see patterns and devise plans that brought clarity to their actions. She reveled in the way her mind worked, like a puzzle clicking into place.

Andrew's strength in combat inspired Asim to hone his skills. Under Andrew's patient guidance, Asim's initial awkwardness transformed into fluidity as he learned to balance strength with precision.

Each practice session was a celebration of progress, the sound of laughter punctuating the clang of steel.

In the afternoons, they ventured into the nearby woods, testing their skills against makeshift dummies Adam had crafted from fallen branches and leaves.

The sun filtered through the trees, casting dappled shadows as they trained, their laughter mingling with the rustle of leaves.

Ananya would often call out encouragement, her voice rising above the hum of nature. "Focus, Asim! You've got this!" Asim would respond with renewed energy, his confidence bolstered by her unwavering support.

As the sun began to dip below the horizon, they gathered around the campfire once more, exhausted but exhilarated. In their shared triumphs and struggles, they learned the true meaning of friendship.

All three of them were scared, but they were scared together.

They discovered that being there for one another—whether through a kind word, a shared laugh, or a supportive gesture—was what truly mattered.

One fateful day, as they prepared for another training session, Adam gathered them for an unexpected challenge. "Today, you will face an obstacle course designed to test your teamwork and adaptability," he announced, his eyes gleaming with excitement.

"Obstacle course?" Ananya echoed, her brow furrowing in concern. "What does that entail?"

Adam grinned. "You'll see. But remember, you must work together to overcome each challenge. Communication and trust are key."

Asim exchanged a nervous glance with Andrew. "I hope it doesn't involve running."

"You can do this," Andrew encouraged, his expression serious but warm. "We've trained for this moment."

The trio set off into the forest, where the course awaited. The sun filtered through the canopy, casting a golden glow on the path ahead. Their surroundings buzzed with energy, the rustling leaves and distant calls of wildlife blending into a soundtrack of nature.

The beauty which will entraps you into your darkness was ready to haunt them.

The first challenge was a series of low-hanging branches and thick roots, a tangled mess that required agility and communication.

Ananya took the lead, guiding Asim and Andrew through the obstacles, her voice steady and encouraging. "Just like we practiced! Watch your step!"

Andrew was surprised at how naturally he navigated the course, the earlier uncertainties fading with each calculated step. Ananya Guided Andrew and Asim followed the same.

Together, they encouraged one another, their camaraderie forging a new kind of strength that felt almost tangible.

As they tackled the next obstacle, a steep hill that required teamwork to scale, Andrew and Asim worked in tandem, hoisting Ananya up before pulling themselves up after her. "Teamwork makes the dream work!" Asim shouted, laughter bubbling in his chest as they reached the top, breathless and exhilarated.

They continued through the course, facing challenges that tested not only their physical abilities but also their mental fortitude.

They encountered pits filled with mud, balancing beams suspended over shallow water, and even a maze of thorny vines. Through it all, they leaned on each other, their trust deepening with every obstacle they conquered.

At the end of the course, the trio collapsed onto the soft grass, gasping for breath and laughing uncontrollably. "That was intense!" Andrew exclaimed, wiping the sweat from his brow.

Ananya grinned, her cheeks flushed with exhilaration. "We did it! I can't believe how far we've come."

Asim, still catching his breath, looked at his friends with newfound admiration. "I never would have imagined I could do something like this. You both pushed me to step out of my comfort zone."

"Together, we can achieve anything," Ananya said, her voice brimming with conviction. She gave a nod to Asim and Andrew, they nodded back.

That day, as they shared their triumphs and laughed over their missteps, they solidified their bond, creating a pact of friendship that would carry them through the dark days ahead.

The fire crackled beside them, a testament to their growing connection, as the stars above twinkled like the dreams they were fighting to protect.

Chapter 8
Shadows of the Unknown

As the days stretched into an unyielding routine, Ananya, and Andrew found themselves entrenched in a cycle of tests and trials. Each challenge brought with it a fresh wave of anxiety, often leaving them on the brink of despair. Though they occasionally emerged victorious, many times they faltered, their spirits dampened.

Yet every time they stumbled, Adam was there, leaping in to lend his strength and guidance.

With the clock ticking down, a palpable fear hung over them—a fear of the unknown, a fear of death. The weight of their impending fate bore down on them like an oppressive fog.

Asim, ever the optimist, tried to lift the mood in their tent one evening. "Come on, guys! Let's lighten up a bit. How about a game?" His voice was hopeful, yet it lacked its usual spark.

Andrew, however, was less inclined to play. "What happens next, though? We can't just keep pretending everything's fine." His brow was furrowed with concern.

Ananya, feeling the same restless uncertainty, chimed in, "Right? Why are we even here? What's the end game?"

Adam, who had been quietly listening, finally spoke. "You're asking the right questions. But the answers lie in understanding the darkness that looms over this kingdom. There is a shadow—a malevolent force known as the Shadow of Night."

The very name sent a shiver down their spines.

"The Shadow of Night traps not just the kingdom, but your minds as well," Adam continued, his voice grave. "It has the power to twist your fears into nightmares, making the world around you crumble to dust."

He paused, allowing the gravity of his words to sink in before continuing. "In our ancient history, there's a prophecy about the 'The Oracle's Heirs.' It speaks of three individuals, each from different time zones, cultures, and backgrounds, yet united by a singular purpose."

Ananya leaned in, captivated. "What's the story?"

Adam began to weave a tale, his voice smooth and rhythmic, echoing the cadence of an ancient rhyme.

"In a time long forgotten, when darkness loomed large,

Three souls were chosen, guided by fate's charge.

From distant lands, each one unique,

Yet together, they were strong, their bond mystique.

One from the mountains, where the sun meets the sky,

One from the valleys, where rivers flow by,

And one from the coast, where the waves softly sing,

Bound by a power, a promise to bring."

The imagery of the rhyme danced in Ananya's mind, painting a picture of strength and unity.

"Together, they fought against the Shadow of Night,

Braving the darkness, igniting their light.

For within them lay a force yet untold,

A power of one that could never grow old."

Adam's voice faded into silence, leaving the trio in thoughtful contemplation.

"Your arrival here mirrors the ancient tale," Adam continued, breaking the quiet. "When you came through the thundering storm and entered the cave, Daikichi sensed a notion. The signs of the past have returned, and we hold on to hope that the shadows will recede."

"But people are losing their minds because of this shadow," remarked, his expression grave. "What if we fail?"

Adam met his gaze with unwavering intensity. "We must not succumb to doubt. Five days have passed since you arrived, and tomorrow we will return to Daikichi. Your journey of fighting the evil begins the day after that."

As the sun set on their final night before embarking on their quest to confront the Shadow of Night, they gathered once more around the fire, their faces illuminated by the warm glow.

"Whatever happens tomorrow," Asim said, his voice steady, "I want you both to know how grateful I am. We've faced so much together, We've learned so much together, and I wouldn't want to do this with anyone else."

"Also I am definetly going to tell my friends this when I wake up from all this." Asim chuckled saying.

Andrew nodded in agreement, and Ananya felt a rush of emotion. "Me too. No matter what comes, we will face it together."

"Together," Andrew added, a fire igniting in his eyes.

"Together," echoed, and they all shared a moment of solidarity, the bonds of friendship stronger than the darkness threatening to envelop them.

As they settled into their tents that night, the bond they had forged felt like an invisible thread connecting their hearts.

They were no longer just three individuals caught in a whirlwind of uncertainty; they were friends—warriors standing together against the encroaching darkness, ready to face whatever awaited them at dawn.

They would confront the Shadow of Night, not as individuals lost in their fears, but as a united front, a trio bound by fate and friendship, ready to reclaim the light.

As sleep began to weave its way into their minds, a sense of peace settled over them. They dreamed of distant lands, united by a common cause, hearts alight with hope, and together they forged a path toward a brighter tomorrow.

Chapter 9
Into the Light

The dawn broke over the horizon, painting the sky with hues of pink and gold. Ananya awoke with a sense of purpose coursing through her veins like fire. Today was the day they would begin their quest to confront the Shadow of Night, a daunting task, but one they would face together.

As they gathered outside their tent, Andrew was busy sharpening the sword he had grown accustomed to wielding.

"It's amusing how few days can change a people." Ananya thought to herself.

The blade gleamed in the morning light, reflecting both his determination and the weight of what lay ahead. Ananya and Asim watched in silence, a sense of camaraderie filling the air.

"Hey, are you ready?" Asim asked, breaking the silence.

Andrew paused, looking up with a serious expression. "I am. But I also know that this is going to be harder than anything we've faced so far."

Ananya placed a reassuring hand on his shoulder. "We've trained and prepared for this. We're not the same people who arrived here five days ago. We've grown stronger."

"Hopefully." Asim commented.

Ananya and Andrew tilted their head in agreement.

As they finished their breakfast, Adam joined them, his presence commanding yet reassuring. "Today marks the beginning of your true journey," he said. "The Shadow of Night will test not just your strength but your resolve, your friendships, and your ability to face the darkness within."

With a nod, they followed Adam as he led them deeper into the forest, the trees towering around them like ancient sentinels.

Each step felt heavier than the last, anticipation mingling with anxiety. The path was shrouded in mist, making the air thick with uncertainty.

"Stay close to each other." Adam instructed, his eyes scanning the surroundings. "The Shadow can manifest in many ways."

As they ventured further, Ananya felt the weight of her fears creeping back. What if they failed? What if the darkness consumed them?

She glanced at her companions, their faces set with determination, and inhaled deeply, steeling her resolve.

After hours of navigating through the misty woods, they arrived at a clearing, the sunlight breaking through the clouds and illuminating the ground. In the center stood a stone altar, covered in vines and moss, a remnant of ancient times. The altar radiated an aura of both danger and significance, and Ananya felt a shiver run down her spine.

"Here lies the replication of the heart of Shadow," Adam explained, his voice low and solemn. "To face it, you must confront not just the darkness outside but the shadows that dwell within yourselves. This is the test of your inner self."

"What do you mean test for my inner self? My inner self is amazing." Asim asked, frowning, his curiosity piqued despite the growing tension.

Adam stepped closer to the altar, the shadows seeming to swirl around him. "The Shadow of Night feeds on your fears, your doubts, and your insecurities. It will try to make you question your worth, your strength, and even your friendships. You must stand firm against it."

Ananya felt her heart race. "What do we do?"

"Each of you must approach the altar and face the Shadow," Adam said. "You will be confronted with your greatest fears, but remember, you are not alone. Your bond will be your strength. Trust in it."

One by one, they stepped forward, their hearts pounding as they stood before the altar.

First was Asim. He took a deep breath, the air heavy with expectation, and placed his hands on the cool stone. Instantly, shadows began to twist and coil around him, whispering his doubts, reminding him of the failures he had faced.

"Why do you think you can fight? You're just a kid playing pretend," the shadows taunted, their voices echoing the insecurity he had felt since childhood—feeling inadequate compared to the older, more experienced warriors around him.

Memories flooded his mind: moments when he hesitated, when his friends had to save him, when he felt like a burden. When he thought he is of no use. Just useless in anyway.

"You don't have an individuality. You are Nothing." That Shadow continues.

"Nooo!! Nooo!!" He sat down, pushing his face in his knees. Mumbling *"Nooooo...Noooo"*

Ananya and Andrew were unable to see anything because of the darkness which has surrounded him.

But then a thought ran through his mind "I can't let you win."

A warm glow ignited within him, fueled by the encouragement he had received from Ananya and the memory of his family's unwavering belief in him. He thought of his younger sister, always looking up to him and drawing strength from his bravery. "No! I'm more than that," he shouted, his voice breaking through the gloom. "I am strong, and I'm not alone!" "I am not alone!" He shouted.

With that declaration, the shadows shrieked and recoiled, dissipating into thin air. Asim stepped back, panting heavily but triumphant, a new light in his eyes.

Ananya and Andrew ran towards him to hold him as he was exhausted.

"Next was Ananya." Adam announced.

"We believe in you. Don't worry we are right here." Andrew tried to comforted Ananya.

She approached the altar, her heart racing as the shadows encircled her. They transformed into images of her past failures—moments of inadequacy and fear that flashed before her eyes like a haunting reel.

"You will never be enough. You can't protect anyone," they hissed, their voices dripping with disdain, conjuring memories of her brother's accident, a moment she had replayed in her mind a thousand times.

Ananya felt her heart drop, fear creeping in like a cold hand gripping her chest. Would she always be unable to save those she loved?

Suddenly there was a laughter, a similar laughter; her brother's laughter, the bond they shared, and the lessons her parents had taught her about courage and resilience. They always reminded her of her unique ability to uplift those around her with her kindness. "I will protect those I love. I am strong, and I refuse to be defined by my fears!"

With a fierce determination, she shattered the darkness, feeling the weight lift from her shoulders as the shadows wailed in protest.

Finally, it was Andrew's turn. He faced the altar, the shadows whispering his deepest insecurities—thoughts of worthlessness and doubt clawing at his mind. "You're not a warrior; you'll fail them all," they sneered, resurrecting memories of past failures—times he had let fear dictate his actions, moments where he felt paralyzed in the face of danger.

Andrew clenched his fists, feeling the heat of determination swell within him.

He recalled his father's words during tough times: "Courage isn't the absence of fear; it's the will to face it." He thought of his mother's unwavering faith in his potential, the way she always encouraged him to follow his heart. "I've come too far to give in! I have my friends with me, and we are stronger together!"

With a roar, he struck the shadows away, his spirit igniting the air around him, pushing back against the encroaching darkness.

As they stepped back, the trio reunited, breaths mingling in the cool morning air. They looked at one another, a fierce sense of unity evident in their eyes, the shadows of their fears now behind them.

"Well done," Adam said, a proud smile gracing his lips. "You faced the darkness and emerged stronger. This is just the beginning."

"Does this mean we're ready?" Ananya asked, hope blooming in her heart, her spirit rekindled.

"More than ready," Adam replied, his voice steady. "Let's hope it all works out; I have believed in you."

With that, they set off once more, determined to reclaim the light for their kingdom. As they ventured deeper into the unknown, the air thickened with anticipation, charged with their resolve. They knew that together, they could face anything.

Their companionship had transformed their fears into strengths, and the memories of their families had ignited an unyielding spirit within them.

Now, as the shadows loomed ahead, they were ready to fight back with everything they had.

Chapter 10
The Chants of Power

After their intense confrontation with the shadows, Ananya, Asim, and Andrew felt invigorated, their spirits high as they retraced their steps back to Daikichi. Each footfall resonated with purpose, and they were filled with a newfound confidence. The path seemed clearer now, the trees whispering encouragement as they passed.

As they approached the familiar clearing where Daikichi awaited them, a sense of urgency enveloped the air. The old sage stood at the altar, his figure silhouetted against the vibrant sky, arms raised in a silent invocation.

"Daikichi!" Ananya called out, her voice filled with hope.

Daikichi turned, his eyes gleaming with a knowing light. "You have returned, and I sense the strength within you has grown. You have faced the darkness and emerged victorious."

"Barely," Asim chimed in with a nervous laugh. "But we did it!"

"Good," Daikichi replied, nodding solemnly. "But your true test lies ahead. To combat the Shadow of Night, you will need more than mere courage. You must be armed with power."

"What do you mean?" Andrew asked, his brows furrowing.

Daikichi gestured for them to gather around him. "I will imbue your weapons with ancient chants that will enhance their power and protect you in the battles to come."

With that, he began to murmur incantations in a melodic voice, each syllable carrying the weight of history and wisdom. The air around them shimmered with energy, and Ananya felt a warm glow envelop her spear, Asim's arrows, and Andrew's sword.

As Daikichi's chants continued, the atmosphere thickened, and sparks of light danced around the weapons, swirling like tiny galaxies. Each chant resonated deeply within their hearts, filling them with a sense of purpose.

"Your weapons will now carry the essence of your spirit," Daikichi explained, his voice a soothing balm against the tension in the air. "They will amplify your strength, granting you the power to overcome the shadows."

Ananya felt the weight of her spear shift in her hands, lighter yet imbued with an unmistakable strength. She glanced at Andrew and Asim, seeing the same realization reflected in their eyes.

Their weapons suddenly started feeling lighter and lighter. Lighter like a feather it was. They were slowing lifting above in the sky approaching each other.

Their corners Clinked.

They got aligned in triangle and started glowing like our brightest star does, Sun. It was beautiful yet powerful.

Daikichi kept chanting.

This was not just about physical weapons; it was about the bond they shared—their friendship was the true source of power.

As Daikichi finished the final chant, a brilliant light enveloped them, and the energy pulsated in waves around the clearing. The sage lowered his arms, a satisfied smile gracing his lips. "You are ready. Trust in your weapons, but more importantly, trust in each other."

"Thank you, Daikichi," Ananya said, her voice filled with gratitude. "We won't let you down."

"Go now, and prepare for the battle against the Shadow. Remember, it is not only the strength of your weapons but the strength of your hearts that will guide you," she replied, a sense of urgency returning to her demeanor.

As they made their way back down the path, the gravity of their mission settled upon them once more. They would face the Shadow, but now they had the tools to fight back, and more importantly, they had each other.

The trio stepped into the misty forest again, determination shining in their eyes. They moved in unison, their hearts beating as one, the chants of power resonating within them.

"Let's do this," Asim said, gripping his arrows tightly.

"Together," Andrew added, his sword gleaming with newfound brilliance.

"Together," Ananya echoed, holding her spear high.

As they were about to venture into the unknown, they knew they were not just fighting for themselves but for the kingdom, for Daikichi, and for the light that had begun to flicker back into their lives.

The darkness awaited them, but they were no longer afraid. Armed with their weapons and strengthened by their friendship, they were ready to confront whatever challenges lay ahead.

Suddenly, without warning, a dark presence surged from the depths of the forest, shadows twisting and coiling like serpents. The followers of the Shadow emerged, their forms grotesque and twisted, eyes glowing with malevolence.

"Fooollllsssss!" one of them hissed, laughter echoing through the clearing. "You think you can defy the Shadow of Night? You will suffer for your insolence!"

Daikichi stepped forward, her voice commanding and resolute. "You dare threaten the prophecy? You will find their strength is far greater than your darkness!"

Within the splits of second there was darkness all around. Not an inch of light could be seen.

Daikichi came forward. With a swift motion, she began chanting a powerful incantation, her voice rising above the chaos.

"Issbiloooreaaaaaaa merrrfeeccctoooooooo!"

The words rang out like a clarion call, a beacon of hope in the encroaching darkness. The darkness faltered, their forms beginning to waver as if the very essence of the shadows was being unraveled.

With a final push, Ananya, Asim, and Andrew unleashed a combined attack—Ananya's spear struck a figure low, Asim's arrows flew like shooting stars, and Andrew's sword cleaved through the air with unmatched fury. The darkness faltered, the form dissipating into the mist as the trio's power surged.

"Now! Now is the time!" Daikichi urged, her voice steady.

But as they were about to leave more darkness started coming towards them. In multiple shapes and forms.

"They all are Followers. Followers, who's minds are entrapped by the Darkness" Daikichi exclaimed.

Fueled by her strength and the bond they shared, the trio pressed forward, their hearts united. They fought as one, their weapons blazing with light, determined to reclaim the kingdom from the clutches.

As the last of the followers fell, a silence descended upon the clearing, the air thick with the remnants of battle. Ananya, Asim, and Andrew stood triumphant, their hearts racing with the thrill of victory.

"Together," they breathed, a collective realization dawning upon them.

Daikichi smiled, pride shining in her eyes. "You have done well. But this is just the beginning of your journey. Remember, the true strength lies not just in your weapons but in the unity of your hearts."

"You will find many more in the forest. Fight as one."

"I can only come this far with you, you go and found the light in this darkness, my ones." Daikichi said with sense of calmness in her voice.

With newfound resolve, they prepared for the next phase of their quest, ready to face whatever darkness awaited them.

"I am lowkey scared." Asim said to Andrew walking towards the forest.

"Me too." Andrew replied.

Three on them were walking ahead, leaving their past behind. They didn't cared they were asleep or awake. They didn't feared what the outcome would be.

They were focused and determined.

Together.

As they ventured deeper into the unknown, they knew they were ready. Armed with their weapons, strengthened by their friendship, and fueled by the memories of their families, they prepared to confront whatever challenges lay ahead.

Chapter 11
The Gathering Storm

As the trio ventured deeper into the forest, a thick fog rolled in, swirling around them like a living entity. The trees loomed overhead, their branches intertwining in a tangled embrace, casting odd shadows on the ground.

Ananya gripped her spear tightly, the chants that Daikichi had imbued within it echoing in her mind, reassuring her yet tinged with the weight of uncertainty.

"Stay close," Andrew said, glancing over his shoulder. "We can't afford to lose each other in here."

As they were moving ahead deep into the forest, the atmosphere felt charged, as if the forest itself was holding its breath, waiting for something to unfold.

Ananya couldn't shake the feeling that they were being watched, the eyes of unseen creatures tracking their every move. A chill crept up her spine, and for a moment, she hesitated, her thoughts spiraling into the abyss of doubt. *What if we can't find our way back? What if we don't wake up at home?*

"What do you think we'll find?" Asim asked, trying to pierce the silence with conversation. "More shadow creatures?"

"Probably," Ananya replied, her voice steady despite the unease creeping into her heart. "But we're prepared now. We can fight back."

Just then, a rustle in the underbrush made them all freeze. Ananya raised her spear defensively, while Andrew drew his sword, and Asim nocked an arrow in his bow.

"Who goes there?" Andrew called out, his voice firm despite the tension.

The rustling intensified, and then a tall figure emerged from the mist—a woman with wild gray hair and tattered robes. Her eyes, however, shone with an otherworldly light.

Beautiful she was like a stream flowing at the night with the reflection of full moon.

"Foolish children," she croaked, her voice like dry leaves crunching underfoot. "You tread a dangerous path."

"Who are you?" Ananya demanded, lowering her spear slightly but still poised for action.

"I am Liora, the Seer of Shadows," the woman replied, her gaze penetrating. "And I have seen what's coming."

"What?" Asim asked, curiosity overcoming his fear.

"The Shadow of Night is no mere creature; it is an ancient evil that feeds on fear and despair," Liora warned, stepping closer. "It seeks to consume all light, and you three are entwined in its dark web."

"Entwined how?" Andrew pressed, his grip tightening on his sword.

"If you are the **Oracle's Heirs**, destined to confront this darkness, but the path ahead is fraught with peril," she said, her tone somber. "You must unite your strengths—your courage, your hope, and your bond of friendship—if you wish to prevail."

Ananya exchanged glances with Asim and Andrew, a silent agreement passing between them. They knew they had to trust this strange woman, but a nagging doubt lingered in the back of their minds.

What if we fail? What if we lose everything we hold dear? *A Chance of Living.*

"What do we need to do?" Ananya asked, determination lacing her voice.

Liora hands reached out near her chest. She closes her eyes and held out her gnarled hands, revealing a shimmering crystal that pulsed with light.

"You must harness the power of this crystal. It holds the essence of hope—your greatest weapon against the shadow. But beware: the closer you get to the Shadow, the stronger your fears will become."

Asim stepped forward, intrigued. "Weapon? Much needed. How do we use it?"

"Keep it close, and let it guide you," Liora instructed. "But remember, when darkness closes in, it will test your resolve. You must not falter."

With that, Liora handed the crystal to Ananya, who accepted it with reverence. The moment it touched her palm, warmth radiated through her, igniting a spark of hope within her heart.

Liora's gaze softened as she explained, "I give this crystal to you, Ananya, because you possess the strongest heart among you. Your spirit shines with resilience and an unwavering belief in the light. You will be the beacon to guide your friends through this darkness. Your doubts and fears will fuel the shadows, but with the crystal, you can transform that energy into strength."

Yet, as she held it, another thought flickered across Ananya's mind—What if this is just an illusion? What if we never escape this nightmare?

"How do we know you are telling the truth. That you are not just a pawn in the Darkness game." Andrew exclaimed.

"Well, you just know. It will be your choice; your instinct to trust me or not. That was my duty which I fulfilled, now you have your duty to do the same." Liora clamly replied.

"Thank you, Liora," Andrew said, his voice sincere. He was taken aback and unfortunately they had no other choice than to just trust their gut. "We'll do our best to protect it."

"I can sesnse, you are still questioning yourself Ananya." Liora sarcastically specified.

"May the light guide you," Liora whispered, retreating back into the mist, her form vanishing as quickly as it had appeared.

With a newfound sense of purpose, the trio pressed on, their spirits bolstered by the encounter. The air was thick with anticipation, and every step felt like a drumbeat echoing the gathering storm. But beneath their bravado lay an undercurrent of fear.

What if we're not strong enough? What if we can't find our way back home?

Each and Every one of them was having doubts, but they were there for each other just walking beside each other.

Suddenly, the ground trembled beneath their feet, and a chilling wind swept through the forest, carrying a whisper that sent shivers down their spines.

"What is that?" Ananya said, her heart racing.

"Ready your weapons," Andrew commanded, the weight of the moment settling in. "Stay close."

As they moved forward, the darkness thickened, and the once vibrant hues of the forest dulled, enveloped in shadows that seemed to twist and writhe.

Then, without warning, shadowy figures emerged from the darkness, their forms indistinct yet menacing. Eyes glowed like embers in the dark, and a low growl reverberated through the air.

"FOLLOWERS! There's too many of them!" Asim shouted, fear creeping into his voice.

"No!" Ananya replied, clutching the crystal tightly. "We will fight them. They are nothing in front of us. Together!"

They ran towards them with all the power they had.

With a unified battle cry, they charged forward, weapons raised, hearts ablaze with the essence of hope. The shadows surged toward them, but this time, they felt an unshakeable bond—their friendship was their shield, and the light within them was their sword.

"Fight!" Andrew shouted, slashing through the darkness, his blade gleaming with power.

Asim released an arrow, its trajectory true, piercing through a shadowy figure, causing it to dissipate into mist.

Ananya thrust her spear forward, channeling the warmth of the crystal, and felt a surge of strength flow through her. The shadows recoiled, a moment of hesitation rippling through their ranks.

"We can do this!" she urged her friends, a fire igniting within her.

Together, they fought, they fought with the chaos, a symphony of defiance against the followers of the darkness. With every strike, they reclaimed a piece of their hope that the person trapped will come out of it, igniting the forest with a brilliant light that pushed back against the encroaching shadows.

They realized that the crystal that Liora gave them was not less than magic. That was transforming shadows into human form. They were able to fight them.

As the battle raged on, they realized that the more they fought, the stronger their bond grew. Fear transformed into courage, despair into hope, and with each passing moment, they became not just warriors but a force of nature—unstoppable, unbreakable.

With the power of the crystal resonating within them and the unwavering strength, they faced the followers of Shadow, ready to reclaim the light.

They were like a clenched fist—unbreakable when united.

Chapter 12
The Heart of Darkness

After the battle with Followers, all three of them were tired, exhausted, and scared. But they decided to keep moving forward.

The air felt charged, as if the forest itself was holding its breath, waiting for something to unfold especially after the sudden outbreak of the followers.

Ananya shivered, sensing unseen creatures watching their every move.

Now she understands that the followers were keeping an eye on them for The Darkness. She recalls feeling the same shiver which she felt while coming out of the cave.

"Do you think we'll find followers again?" Asim asked tried to ease the tension "More shadow creatures? Or someone like Liora?"

"We're ready this time. Whatever we encounter with." Ananya replied.

"Just stay focused and stay close." Andrew added.

They can sense something.

Shh; Andrew indicated by hand gestures.

They can listen the swishing of winds, but not rhythemetically. It was something unusal. Suddenly there was mist, the mist surrounded them like a wrapping paper covering them in his arm. A cold sense in their heart.

All three froze suddenly. Ananya raised her spear, Andrew unsheathed his sword, and Asim nocked an arrow, prepared for anything.

Then, the fog thickened, and a figure began to move—not just creeping along the forest floor but taking shape, twisting into sinister figure. Its eyes gleamed like embers in the dark, and a low growl resonated through the air.

They can hear a growling sound.

The fear and anxiety crumbles in Ananya's heart, like her heart was about to be broken into pieces. She suddenly wanted to haul in sadness. Like she wanted to scream like no other.

"It must be the Shadow of Night," Ananya whispered, her heart racing.

"Ready your weapons," Andrew commanded, tightening his grip on his sword. "Stay close. We fight as one."

The shadows surged toward them, writhing and swirling like a tide of darkness. Its form flickered, indistinct yet menacing, as if feeding off the fear that lingered in the air.

"oh my god this is something else!" Asim shouted, panic creeping into his voice.

Ananya stepped forward, clutching her spear. "We can't let him intimidate us."

Its eyes glowed and it disappeared for the moment. There was this pin drop silence again.

"Youuuuu challlleeenged meee?" Something Hissed.

"Chaallenggeedd theee Shhaaddoowww Itself."

The Darkness came out suddenly like a wind getting inside of their mind with the help of mist. In the meanwhile it also broke down its body into many disfigured shadows.

The fears reclaimed their mind chanting the darkest things that they didn't want to hear.

"You are not enough."

"You jokesters"

"You are a burden to your family"

"You should die."

"You have achieved nothing."

They were lost in their own thoughts, a heavy weight of inadequacy pressing down on them. The world felt dim and distant, as if a curtain had fallen, blocking out any light. Suddenly, darkness enveloped them, filled with echoes of laughter and mockery that pierced through their mind.

Every jest felt like a reminder of their flaws, amplifying the feeling of being alone in a crowd. They wished for connection but felt like an outsider, as if they were invisible yet painfully visible at the same time.

Hope felt like a distant memory, overshadowed by a deep sense of worthlessness that wrapped around them like a heavy blanket. In that moment, the laughter of others became a haunting reminder of their struggles, deepening the shadows that clouded their heart.

Suddenly in the middle of mockery Ananya heard his brother's laugh and giggles again. Her younger brother's innocent sarcasm, which gave her strength.

"No we are more than enough" Ananya tried whiling gaining her consciousness.

"WE ARE ENOUGHHH" Ananya Shouted out of her lungs.

After hearing Ananya's voice, Asim and Andrew slowly regained their senses, the fog of confusion lifting. They grasped the situation once more, adrenaline surging through their veins.

With fierce determination, Andrew tightened his grip on his sword and charged at the shadow, shouting, "Aaaaahhhhhhh!" as he unleashed all his strength in a powerful swing.

Asim stumbled to the ground, but Ananya quickly rushed to his side, helping him to his feet. The three of them rose, ready to fight like the true warriors they were, united.

The forest trembled with the clash between light and dark. Each strike they made felt like a reclamation—a small piece of themselves pulled back from the abyss.

Yet, the Shadow of Night pressed harder, growing more aggressive, as if determined to extinguish their light.

"They're feeding on our fear!" Ananya shouted, her voice cutting through the chaos. "We have to fight with everything—our courage, our hope, and our trust in each other!"

Andrew grinned through the sweat on his brow. "Then let's give him hell."

Asim loosed another arrow, and Ananya thrust her spear into a swirling mass of shadows. She felt something, she intuitively put the crystal into the shadow.

It was like prism, light shining through everywhere.

Ananya felt confident, the warmth within her grew, burning brighter as she fought. The Shadow recoiled, faltering for the first time.

"This is working!" Andrew shouted, slashing through another figure. "Keep going!"

The trio fought with unwavering resolve, their movements synchronized like a symphony of defiance. Each strike resonated with the power of their bond, a beacon of light pushing back against the night.

Asim's smirks echoed through the forest, mingling with Andrew's shouts and Ananya's fierce determination.

The Shadows began to waver, their once-mighty presence weakening. The forest, too, seemed to respond—vibrant hues returning to the trees as if waking from a nightmare.

"We're doing it!" Asim cheered, his arrow flying straight through the heart of a shadow.

But the Shadow wasn't finished yet. It coalesced into a figure. Its form twisted and roiled, eyes burning with malice as it loomed over them.

Ananya gritted her teeth, feeling the weight of the moment settle in her chest. "This is it. Together, one final push!"

The trio closed ranks, drawing strength from each other. Andrew's sword gleamed with defiance, Asim's bowstring hummed with anticipation, and Ananya's spear burned with unyielding hope.

With a unified cry, they charged at the Shadow of Night. The darkness lashed out, but their light was stronger—brighter. The force of their friendship and courage overwhelmed the shadow, unraveling it with every strike.

Andrew's blade cut deep, splitting the darkness apart. Asim's arrows struck true, piercing through its core. Ananya, with one final thrust of her spear, unleashed the full power of Daikichi's chants, igniting the night with a radiant burst of light.

The Shadow of Night shrieked, its form disintegrating into tendrils of mist, carried away by a gust of wind. The forest erupted with energy, the oppressive weight of fear lifting as sunlight broke through the canopy, bathing everything in warmth.

For a moment, they stood still, catching their breath, disbelief mingling with triumph.

"We did it…" Asim whispered, awe in his voice.

"WE DID IT!" He then shouted.

Ananya looked at her friends, a smile breaking across her face. "Together."

Andrew raised his sword high, laughing with unrestrained joy. "We faced the darkness—and won? Who knew?" "That to in my dreams…haha" Andrew Chuckled.

"This is the because we are the most Alive we have ever been."

"We are *Unconsciously Alive.*" Ananya had a smile while saying that.

They embraced, their hearts light and spirits soaring, knowing they had fought not just for survival but for each other. The forest around them was alive again, the echoes of their victory etched into every leaf and branch.

But even in their triumph, Ananya knew this was only the beginning. The Shadow of Night had fallen, but their journey wasn't over.

"We need to find Daikichi," she said, her voice steady with purpose. "We have to tell her what happened."

Andrew nodded, wiping the sweat from his brow. "Let's go home."

As they made their way through the brightened forest, the warmth of the sun guided their path. Though challenges still lay ahead, they knew they could face anything—together.

Bound by hope, courage, and the strength of their friendship, they had become more than warriors. They were a force of light—and their journey had only just begun.

Chapter 13
Ancestral Guardians

As the trio made their way back to Daikichi, a sense of accomplishment swelled within them, mingling with the anticipation of what lay ahead. The shadows had retreated, but Ananya couldn't shake the feeling that a greater challenge awaited them.

The forest, once filled with dread, now resonated with the soft melodies of nature, as if celebrating their victory. Sunlight streamed through the leaves, casting a golden glow that seemed to imbue the world with newfound hope.

Upon reaching Daikichi's encampment, the wise elder was already waiting for them, her expression a mixture of relief and pride. The camp was adorned with sacred symbols and protective wards, their intricate patterns shimmering faintly in the dappled light.

"You've returned," she said, a hint of a smile tugging at her lips. "And I see the light in your eyes. You faced the Shadow of Night and emerged victorious."

"We did, Daikichi!" Ananya exclaimed, her heart racing with excitement. "But we sensed that this was just the beginning. There's more darkness to confront, isn't there?"

Daikichi nodded, her gaze turning serious. "Indeed, the battle against darkness is never truly over. The Shadow of Night may have been vanquished, but its influence lingers, and other forces may rise in its place."

Asim's brow furrowed with concern. "What kind of forces? Are they stronger than the Shadow?"

"There are ancient beings known as the Wraiths," Daikichi explained, her voice low and steady. "Creatures born of the void, they thrive on fear and despair. If left unchecked, they will seek to plunge the kingdom back into chaos."

Andrew clenched his fists, determination igniting within him. "We can't let that happen! We must prepare for whatever comes next."

Daikichi gestured for them to sit around a fire that crackled warmly, the flames casting flickering shadows on their faces. "Your strength lies in your unity, but you must also embrace your individual powers. Each of you possesses a unique gift, one that will be crucial in the trials ahead."

Ananya felt a flicker of hope. "What do we need to do?"

"First, we must keep calm" Daikichi instructed. "You will learn to harness your abilities, to channel your fears into strength. And you must also uncover the secrets of your past, for the key to defeating the Wraiths lies within you."

"Secrets of our past?" Asim echoed, intrigued yet puzzled. "What do you mean?"

"You three are not just chosen at random," Daikichi said, her gaze piercing through them. "Your backgrounds and cultures hold significance in this battle. Each of you carries a piece of history that ties you to this kingdom and its fate."

Daikichi leaned closer, her voice dropping to a whisper, as if revealing a sacred truth. "In ancient times, three guardians stood against the forces of darkness. They were bound by a powerful connection that transcended time and space, existing in different realms yet forming a triangle—a sacred geometric shape that channels energy and power. You must learn about their stories, as you are the reincarnations of those guardians."

Ananya's mind raced, trying to piece together the fragments of her past. "What should we do?"

Daikichi stood, the air around her shimmering with a quiet intensity. "Tonight, I will guide you through the Ritual of Remembrance. It will help you unlock the memories that lie dormant within you, revealing the connections to your ancestors and their sacrifices."

The trio exchanged glances, a mix of excitement and apprehension coursing through them. "We're ready," Andrew declared, his resolve unwavering.

As night fell, the encampment was filled with a hushed reverence. Daikichi led them to a sacred clearing, illuminated by glowing stones that pulsed with a gentle light, arranged in a triangular formation that mirrored the ancient guardians' coordinates. The air buzzed with energy, and the forest seemed to hold its breath in anticipation.

"Close your eyes," Daikichi instructed, her voice calm and soothing. "Breathe deeply, and let the past flow through you."

Ananya felt the warmth of the crystal still pulsing in her hands, and she focused on its glow. With each breath, she sensed the intertwining of her present and past, the stories of her ancestors weaving together with her own.

Visions began to dance in her mind—images of her grandmother, a fierce warrior in her youth, standing strong against adversities, wielding a sword that glimmered like the stars. She felt the weight of her legacy pressing down, urging her to rise.

The vision shifted, revealing her ancestors standing united against a dark force, their spirits intertwining in a dance of defiance, creating a protective barrier that shimmered with light.

Asim was next, his brow furrowing in concentration. He saw flashes of his childhood, moments of laughter with friends and family, but also shadows of fear. He felt the struggles of his people, their resilience against oppression, surging forth, empowering him.

He envisioned his ancestors forging weapons in the fires of rebellion, their spirits whispering tales of hope that echoed through generations.

Andrew's eyes flew open in surprise. He recalled stories of his ancestors, legendary guardians of light, their valor and courage echoing through time. He saw their triumphs and their sacrifices, the burdens they bore in their fight against the darkness.

He felt their strength coursing through his veins, igniting a fire of determination, and he realized that their legacy lived on within him.

"Embrace these memories," Daikichi whispered, her voice blending with the murmurs of the forest. "They are a part of you. Use them as your guiding light."

As they absorbed the weight of their histories, the glowing stones around them pulsed brighter, filling the clearing with radiant energy.

Ananya felt the bond between them strengthen, their shared memories forging a connection deeper than any they had experienced before.

In that moment, they understood: they were not just three individuals caught in a dark fate; they were part of a larger tapestry, woven with courage, sacrifice, and hope. The strength of their ancestors would guide them through the trials that lay ahead.

When the ritual ended, Daikichi looked at them, pride shining in her eyes. "You have awakened the power within you. This knowledge will be your greatest weapon against the Wraiths."

Ananya said, her voice steady. "We won't let you down."

"We will face whatever comes next," Andrew added, determination etched across his features.

Daikichi nodded, a sense of approval washing over her. "Then prepare yourselves. The storm is gathering, and it will take all of you—together—to face it."

As they made their way back to the camp, Ananya, Asim, and Andrew felt a renewed sense of purpose. The path ahead would be fraught with challenges, but they were no longer just three frightened souls.

They were warriors united by friendship, armed with the strength of their pasts and the resolve to protect their future.

Together, they would stand against the void that threatened this world, bound by the legacy of their ancestors and the powerful triangle they formed, each point representing their unique strengths converging into one unstoppable force.

Chapter 14
The Final Confrontation

The dawn broke with an ominous hue, the sky a swirling canvas of grays and purples. The first light of day struggled to penetrate the thick clouds, casting a muted glow over the forest.

Ananya, Asim, and Andrew gathered their weapons, the weight of their responsibilities heavier than ever. Each weapon gleamed with an ethereal light—a sword forged from the remnants of fallen stars, a bow strung with the threads of time, and a staff that pulsed with the heartbeat of the earth.

Today marked the culmination of their journey—the final confrontation against the Wraiths that threatened their world.

The trio exchanged determined glances, each aware that they were not merely fighting for their survival but for the legacy of their ancestors who had once wielded power in their time.

As they approached Daikichi's tent, the elder stood waiting, her silhouette framed against the vibrant colors of the awakening day. Her expression was a mix of solemnity and hope, a testament to the trials they had overcome.

"This is it, my young warriors," she said, her voice resonating with a quiet strength that filled the air around them. "You have trained, remembered, and united. Now you must face the darkness."

"What's the plan, Daikichi?" Asim asked, his tone a blend of eagerness and apprehension, his eyes flickering with the fire of determination.

"First, we must locate the source of the Wraiths' power," Daikichi explained, her voice steady and commanding. "It lies deep within the Forgotten Caverns, a place where light rarely penetrates. You will need to work together, combining your abilities to navigate the darkness."

Andrew clenched his fists, determination flooding through him. "We're ready for this. We'll protect each other."

"Remember," Daikichi cautioned, her gaze piercing through them, "the Wraiths feed off fear. If you let doubt creep in, they will exploit it. Trust in yourselves and in one another."

With those words echoing in their minds, the trio set off towards the caverns, the forest eerily silent around them.

The path twisted and turned, the trees looming like ancient sentinels guarding the secrets of the kingdom. The atmosphere thickened, charged with the energy of the impending battle.

As they entered the caverns, an unsettling chill enveloped them, the air thick with anticipation. The walls shimmered with an ethereal glow, casting visions shadows that danced around them like specters.

Ananya and Asim felt their heart race, echoing the doubts of generations past.

"I am scared as well." Andrew urged, his voice steady but low, drawing strength from their shared resolve. "I thought Darkness would be the one we have to fought"

"It's like a video game. Some suspense. I don't want to be in that. I don't even like it." Asim exclaimed.

"Well, we have to trust our instincts remember" Ananya recalled.

"One last step forward?" Ananya questioned both raising her eyebrows.

"One last step forward." Both whispered synchronizing their voices.

As they ventured deeper, the glow from the crystals dimmed, and the oppressive void pressed in on them. Suddenly, a cold laugh echoed through the cavern, reverberating off the jagged walls.

"Ah, the chosen ones," a voice hissed, dripping with malice. "How brave of you to venture into my domain. Do you truly believe you can defeat me?"

The Wraith materialized before them, a swirling mass of shadows with eyes that glinted like shards of ice, each one a reflection of their deepest fears. Ananya felt a chill run down her spine, but she forced herself to stand tall.

"We're here to end your reign of terror," she declared, her voice stronger than she felt, emboldened by the memories of her ancestors—a lineage of warriors who had once protected the realm with unwavering courage.

"Such bravado!" The Wraith cackled, its form shifting like smoke. "But you are nothing compared to the shadows that lie within. Your fears will be your undoing."

With a wave of its hand, the Wraith conjured dark tendrils that reached for them, wrapping around their ankles, pulling them into the abyss. Ananya gasped as despair flooded her mind again, images of failure and loss swirling around her—visions of her grandmother, a fierce warrior in her youth, falling in battle, a fate she feared for herself and her friends.

As the Wraith materialized before them, its form coalesced into a swirling mass of shadows, a dark tempest that seemed to absorb the very light around it.

Its eyes glinted like shards of ice, piercing through the gloom, each glimmer reflecting the trio's deepest fears—visions of failure, despair, and loss dancing in the corners of their minds. Ananya felt a cold sweat trickle down her spine as dread wrapped around her heart.

"We're here to end your reign of terror!" Ananya declared, forcing strength into her voice, her weapon clutched tightly in her hands. The sword, forged from the remnants of fallen stars, glimmered faintly, as if resonating with her resolve.

"Such bravado!" The Wraith cackled, the sound echoing off the cavern walls, reverberating through the air like a sinister symphony. "But you are nothing compared to the shadows that lie within. Your fears will be your undoing." It raised a hand, and with a flick of its wrist, dark tendrils erupted from the shadows, slithering toward them like serpents hungry for prey.

Ananya gasped as the tendrils wrapped around her ankles, icy fingers constricting and pulling her toward the abyss. Panic surged within her, a wave of despair crashing over her as visions of her past flooded her mind—the faces of her ancestors lost in battles against darkness, their cries echoing through time.

"Ananya!" Andrew shouted, his voice sharp and urgent. He lunged forward, struggling against the encroaching shadows that sought to ensnare him as well. "Fight it! Remember who you are!"

Asim, with his bow at the ready, notched an arrow strung with threads of time, aiming for the heart of the darkness. "We won't let it take you!" he vowed, his voice steady despite the fear clawing at his chest.

The air crackled with tension as the Wraith's laughter rang out, mocking and cruel. "Ah, the power of friendship! How quaint! But you will find it means nothing here!" The Wraith waved its hand again, and more tendrils surged forward, this time wrapping around Andrew's wrists, pulling him back.

"Ananya!" Andrew shouted, struggling against the dark tendrils that threatened to ensnare him as well. "Fight it! Remember who you are!"

The echoes of her ancestors' strength rang in her ears, reminding her of the legacy she carried, the whispers of her grandmother and her unyielding spirit urging her to rise. Summoning her courage, Ananya focused on the light within her, pushing against the shadows that threatened to consume her.

"No!" Ananya shouted, summoning every ounce of her will. Memories of her grandmother's strength surged within her, the legacy of the warriors who had fought before her igniting a fire in her soul. "I am not afraid!" With a sudden surge of energy, she focused on the light within her, the warmth that had always been her shield against despair.

With a determined scream, she pushed against the shadows, breaking free from the tendrils' grasp. The darkness writhed as she surged forward, her sword glowing brighter, illuminating the cavern with a radiant light. "Together!" she urged, her heart racing as she reached for her friends.

Asim and Andrew, sensing the shift in her energy, quickly rallied beside her. They joined hands, forming an unbreakable **Triangle**, their collective strength amplifying the light. Like Prism, the light is distributing its way.

Their weapons pulsed with vibrant energy, casting away the shadows that threatened to consume them.

The Wraith hissed, its form flickering as the light pushed against it, revealing glimpses of the horror lurking within—the lost souls it had devoured, trapped in a never-ending cycle of torment. "Your bond is strong," it spat, the anger in its voice palpable. "But it will not save you!"

With a roar, the Wraith lunged at them, shadows swirling around it like a storm, dark tendrils reaching out to ensnare the trio once more. But Ananya, Asim, and Andrew stood firm, their hearts synchronized in defiance.

"Now!" Andrew shouted, determination blazing in his eyes. In that moment, they unleashed a surge of energy that flowed through them, a brilliant light erupting from their joined hands, shooting forth like a comet cutting through the night sky.

The light collided with the Wraith, illuminating the cavern in a blinding brilliance that momentarily pushed back the shadows. The Wraith shrieked, a sound of pure rage and despair that echoed through the depths, its form flickering like a dying flame. "No!" it howled, the shadows around it convulsing in agony.

But the power of their friendship and companionship proved too strong. As the light enveloped the Wraith, it writhed and twisted, the darkness beginning to dissolve like mist under the morning sun.

The echoes of their ancestors' strength surged through them, reinforcing their resolve as they pressed on, pouring every ounce of their energy into the strike.

"Together!" Ananya cried, her voice cutting through the chaos. With one final push, they directed their combined strength toward the Wraith. The light exploded forth, a beacon of hope piercing the heart of the darkness.

"No!" the Wraith shrieked, its voice filled with fury and disbelief as the light consumed it, unraveling its form until it was nothing more than a whisper in the wind.

The cavern shook, the walls trembling as the shadows melted away, leaving only a warm glow in their wake.

Breathless and trembling, Ananya, Asim, and Andrew stood together in the aftermath, their hearts racing in unison.

There was a sweetness in silence.

The oppressive darkness that had loomed over them was gone, replaced by a profound silence, the air now charged with the energy of victory.

"We did it," Ananya whispered, disbelief mingling with joy as tears of relief streamed down her cheeks.

"We faced the darkness and emerged victorious," Andrew added, a smile breaking through his earlier worry, the weight of fear lifting from his shoulders.

Asim laughed, a sound of genuine relief and newfound strength. "And we didn't even break a sweat! Well, maybe a little," he added, trying to lighten the moment as they stepped out of the cavern into the radiance of the transformed world outside.

Breathless and trembling, Ananya, Asim, and Andrew stood together, their hearts racing in unison.

"We did it," Ananya whispered, disbelief mingling with joy, her spirit ignited by the triumph of their unity.

"We faced the darkness and emerged victorious," Andrew added, a smile breaking through his earlier worry, the warmth of hope wrapping around them like a cloak.

Asim laughed, a sound of relief and newfound strength. "And we didn't even break a sweat! Well, maybe a little."

As they made their way out of the caverns, the world around them began to shift. The oppressive atmosphere lifted, replaced by warmth and light.

They emerged into a landscape transformed—flowers blooming in vibrant colors, the air filled with the sweet scent of renewal, and the sky radiant with hues of gold and azure.

Returning to Daikichi, they were met with cheers from the gathered townsfolk, a wave of joy washing over them. The elder's eyes sparkled with pride as she approached them. "You have done the impossible. You faced the shadows and brought light back to our kingdom."

"This is it then, thank god." Asim whispered to Ananya and Andrew.

"No more surprises for us." Andrew commented and all three started laughing.

"We couldn't have done it without each other," Ananya replied, glancing at her friends, her heart swelling with gratitude. "We're stronger together."

"And you always will be," Daikichi affirmed, placing her hands on their shoulders, her voice imbued with wisdom. "The bond you've forged will guide you through any darkness that may come."

With newfound strength and unity, Ananya, Asim, and Andrew looked to the horizon, where the sun was beginning to rise, casting away the remnants of night.

Their journey had transformed them—not just into warriors but into lifelong friends, bound by their shared experiences and the light they carried within.

As they stood together, ready to face whatever lay ahead, they knew one thing for certain: no matter the challenge, they would always find their way back to the light.

Chapter 15
The Dawn of New Beginnings

As Ananya, Asim, and Andrew emerged from the caverns, they stood in awe of the breathtaking landscape that greeted them. The sky was painted in vibrant hues of orange and pink, the sun breaking over the horizon, casting a warm glow over the fields of blooming flowers. Each petal shimmered with dew, reflecting the light in a dazzling display.

"This is incredible!" Asim exclaimed, his voice a mix of wonder and excitement. He spun in a circle, taking in the beauty around them. "I can't believe we actually did it!"

Andrew nodded, a smile stretching across his face. "And we survived! What a team we made."

Ananya felt a rush of joy swell within her. "We didn't just survive; we triumphed. Together." She looked at her friends, the bond they forged stronger than any darkness they had faced.

As they settled on a grassy knoll, a sense of peace enveloped them. The world around them buzzed with life—birds sang sweet melodies, and the gentle rustle of leaves danced with the soft breeze.

"I don't want this moment to end," Ananya said, gazing out at the horizon. "It feels like a dream."

"Speaking of dreams, let's connect, just in case this is all a dream," Andrew suggested.

"But we have to memorize it here bro, no follows or unfollow. Oh! You will love my content." Asim Exclaimed.

"We should exchange social media handles. If we wake up in our lives, we'll still have a way to reach each other."

"Great idea!" Asim said enthusiastically. They quickly shared their usernames, started memorizing them, laughter and excitement filling the air.

As the radiant light enveloped Ananya, the air shimmered around her, and suddenly, the clearing brightened with energy. Daikichi stepped forward, her presence commanding yet gentle, followed closely by Adam and the villagers who had once been shrouded in darkness.

The villagers looked different now; their eyes sparkled with life and hope, unburdened from the weight of despair that had once held them captive. They filled the clearing, their expressions a mixture of awe and gratitude, surrounding the trio with warmth and support.

"Look!" Asim exclaimed, his eyes wide with wonder. "They're free!"

"Yes, they are," Daikichi said, her voice resonating with pride. "Your bravery and unity have not only vanquished the Wraiths but have also awakened the spirits of those who had been lost in shadows."

Adam stepped forward, a radiant smile illuminating his face. "We owe you our lives," he said, his voice filled with emotion. "Your courage has brought us back to the light. We were lost, but now we can finally see the beauty of our world again."

As Ananya entered her details, a thought crossed her mind. "What is this place, Daikichi? We've fought bravely and faced the darkness, but we still don't know where we are."

Daikichi, standing nearby, smiled at them, her eyes twinkling with a mysterious light. "You are in Animrew, a realm born from the very essence of your spirits. It's a place where magic and warmth intertwine. It was created from your names, Ananya, Asim, and Andrew—ANIMREW."

The trio exchanged stunned glances, their minds racing with the significance of the revelation. "That's amazing!" Ananya gasped. "A place made from us!"

"Yes," Daikichi nodded, her expression turning more solemn. "But remember, every magic has its time, and every journey must come to a close."

As Ananya absorbed the beauty of Animew, she felt a gentle warmth wash over her, wrapping around her like a comforting embrace. It was as if the very essence of the realm was recognizing her presence. She closed her eyes, letting the sensation of floating envelop her, a blissful weightlessness that made her feel at peace.

Ananya, still floating in the warmth of Animew, felt a surge of joy in her heart. "We couldn't have done it without each other," she replied, her voice carrying across the clearing. "Together, we faced the darkness and emerged victorious."

The villagers began to cheer, their voices rising in a harmonious chorus of celebration. It was a sound that echoed through the forest, a melody of unity and strength, weaving a tapestry of hope that wrapped around them all.

"Thank you, Daikichi," Andrew said, turning to the elder with gratitude in his eyes. "For guiding us and believing in us. You taught us to harness our strengths."

Daikichi smiled warmly, her eyes twinkling with wisdom. "You have always had the power within you, my young warriors. I merely helped you see it. The strength of your bond and the love you share are what truly vanquished the darkness."

Adam stepped forward again, his voice steady and clear. "We have all felt the shadows in our lives. The fear, the despair. But now, thanks to you three, we can choose to embrace the light. We are free to build a future together, a future filled with magic and warmth, just like this place."

Ananya, feeling the collective energy of hope surrounding her, spoke up. "We should celebrate our victory and the new beginnings that await us! Let's create a tradition to honor this day—the day we broke the chains of fear and chose to stand united."

The villagers nodded in agreement, excitement buzzing in the air. They began to gather around, sharing stories of resilience and courage, weaving their experiences together into a beautiful narrative of triumph.

As the sun rose higher, painting the landscape in brilliant colors, the atmosphere became infused with laughter and joy. Ananya, Asim, and Andrew joined the villagers, feeling a deep sense of belonging. They danced and celebrated, their spirits lifted by the knowledge that they had changed the fate of not only their own lives but the lives of everyone in Animew.

In that moment, as they twirled and sang, Ananya felt the warmth of their unity wrap around her like a comforting embrace. She knew that they were all now connected—not just through the battles they fought but through the love and light they had ignited together.

As the festivities continued, Daikichi stood at the edge of the clearing, a soft smile gracing her lips. She watched the three young warriors and the villagers come together, knowing that their journey was just beginning. They had faced darkness and emerged victorious, but new adventures awaited them—adventures that would continue to strengthen their bond and illuminate their path.

With the dawn of a new day in Animew, the future shone brightly ahead of them, filled with promise and the magic of friendship.

"It's time," Daikichi said softly, her voice echoing like a soothing breeze. "Remember, Ananya's time zone is first. That means her sun rises before any of yours. It's her time to depart."

"Wait! This is happening. For real!" Asim said, a hint of panic creeping into his voice. "But that's not enough time!"

Ananya smiled, the warmth still surrounding her like a protective cocoon. "It's enough. I'll carry this place and all of you in my heart. No matter where we are, we'll always be connected."

As the warmth intensified, Ananya felt herself lifting gently off the ground, the colors of Animew swirling around her, merging into a tapestry of light. Her friends reached out, their hands brushing against hers, a final connection before she began to drift away.

"Don't forget us!" Andrew shouted, his voice filled with emotion.

"I could never," Ananya replied, her heart swelling with love for her friends. "You'll always be a part of me."

With that, she was enveloped in a brilliant light, and as the world around her faded, she held onto the promise of reunion, knowing that the bonds they forged in Animew would transcend time and space.

"See you on the other side," she added, determination lighting her eyes.

Epilogue
A New Beginning

"Ananya, wake up! It's time for your office!"

Morning was dawned bright and clear, sunlight streaming through Ananya's window like a warm embrace. The golden rays cascaded into her room, casting playful shadows that danced across the walls. As she stirred awake to her mother's familiar call, a sense of warmth enveloped her, a stark contrast to the shadows they had faced just a day before.

Blinking against the brightness, she slowly sat up, letting the light fill her senses.

"It was just a dream afterall" She thought to herself. But no dreams feel this real. She was confused, very confused. And tired! But there was a sense of calmness in her mind.

Memories of their adventure flooded her mind—the trials they had overcome, the bond they had forged, and the exhilarating rush of standing together against the Wraith.

But a nagging feeling tugged at her heart. What if it had all been a dream? Could such a fantastical journey exist in reality? Ananya shook her head, dispelling the thought.

She was anxious and confused but just then, after hours of confusion, her phone buzzed on the nightstand, pulling her from her reverie.

It was a message from Andrew: "Can't believe we're back! I woke up in my own bed, but it feels surreal.

You okay? Sorry, Do you know me? Dreammate? Remember much?"

A smile spread across her face as she quickly typed back: "Hell yes! I'm good! It feels like a dream. I was so confused. I am glad it was not just a dream. I miss you both already! Did you hear from Asim? I am worried."

Hours later, her phone buzzed again—this time from Asim: "Hey! Just woke up. Thank god I am not dead. Congratulations cause you are not dead too! Let's navigate a meet up later this month and talk about everything. I have so much to share!"

Excitement surged through Ananya as they quickly organized a meet-up at a Cassel-themed café, a local spot known for its cozy nooks and vibrant décor, nearby her space. The café was adorned with whimsical artwork and had a cheerful ambiance that mirrored their newfound hope. Ananya felt a rush of anticipation as she got ready, her heart racing at the thought of reuniting with her friends.

When they arrived at the café, the atmosphere was alive with laughter and conversation. As soon as Andrew and Asim spotted her, they waved enthusiastically. Ananya rushed over, enveloping them in a warm, tight hug, feeling the reassurance of their friendship wrap around her like a protective cloak.

"It's so good to see you!" Andrew exclaimed, his eyes sparkling with enthusiasm, the remnants of their shared adventure still visible in his expression.

Asim grinned widely, his energy infectious. "This place! I can't believe we actually did that! We fought the

Shadow of Night and now we're back in our own world!"

They settled into a corner booth, the sun casting a golden hue over their table. The aroma of freshly brewed coffee and sweet pastries filled the air, creating a comforting atmosphere. As they sipped their drinks, they exchanged stories about their lives since returning home, sharing snippets of everyday adventures and catching up on what they had missed.

"I feel like we've changed," Ananya mused, glancing between her friends, a pensive look crossing her face. "That journey brought us so much closer. I don't think I could have faced those challenges without you both."

"Same here," Andrew nodded, his expression thoughtful. "It's like we're bound by something deeper now. We fought together, and that's not something you forget."

"Totally," Asim agreed, his enthusiasm bubbling over. "And I think we should keep that connection alive. We should have regular meet-ups to stay in touch and support each other."

As the conversation flowed, they laughed about their experiences, recounting the hilarious moments and the scary ones. Ananya felt a sense of peace wash over her; it was as if they had picked up right where they left off, the bond they shared now even stronger.

As the days turned into weeks, the trio maintained their bond, connecting through social media, video calls, and regular hangouts. They shared memes, photos, and memories of their adventure, often reminiscing about their time in Animew. Their friendship flourished, deepening with every conversation.

One evening, as they sat together at their favorite café, Ananya brought up an idea. "What if we start a blog? We can document our experiences and even inspire others to face their own challenges. I think it would be amazing to share our story."

Andrew's eyes lit up, his excitement evident. "That's a fantastic idea! We can include tips on facing fears and overcoming obstacles—maybe even a section on our adventure."

Asim nodded eagerly. "Let's do it! It can be a platform for us to encourage others and keep our story alive."

And so, The Oracle's Heirs Blog was born. They poured their hearts into it, sharing tales of friendship, bravery, and the power of unity. They crafted posts that blended their real-life experiences with the fantastical elements of their adventure, painting vivid pictures for their readers. As their blog gained traction, they connected with others who had faced their own shadows, creating a community of support and inspiration.

Years passed, and the trio continued to cherish their bond. They celebrated milestones together—birthdays, graduations, and new jobs—supporting each other through challenges, laughter, and tears. They traveled to new places, their adventures expanding beyond the kingdom they once fought to save, each trip strengthening their connection.

Though they had returned to their normal lives, they knew that the light they had ignited within themselves would never fade. Their journey had taught them that no darkness could extinguish the bonds of friendship, and they were forever grateful for the experiences that had brought them together.

In their hearts, they carried the memories of their adventure—the laughter, the fears, and the triumphs.

Ananya often found herself reflecting on those moments, the shadows they conquered, and the warmth that followed. Together, they knew they could face anything that life threw their way.

As they stood together, ready to embrace whatever lay ahead, Ananya felt a sense of purpose envelop her. The story of their friendship was just beginning, and they were excited to see where it would lead them next.

About the Author

Bhumika Goswami

Bhumika Goswami is an accomplished author and a seasoned Cloud Engineer specializing in Azure and AWS. With extensive experience in managing cloud migration projects across diverse industries, she possesses a deep understanding of modern technology and its impact on productivity.

As an author, Bhumika has published two books—Seasons of Life and Minimal | न्यूनतम. Her writing reflects her passion for literature and the complexities of human experiences.

Seasons of Life offers insights into the beautiful rollercoaster ride of emotions and choices that shape our lives.

In contrast, Minimal | न्यूनतम is a bilingual pocketbook that presents profound reflections in both Hindi and English, celebrated for its simplicity and emotional depth. Bhumika's ability to weave relatable narratives resonates with readers, inviting them to explore the intricacies of life through her words.

For her penning down something is a way of venting out emotion. Writing has a power to initialize change and awareness. That's what her aim is.

Initializing Awareness.

Milton Keynes UK
Ingram Content Group UK Ltd.
UKHW031634201124
451457UK00006B/57